What readers say about Harlequin Romances

"Your books are the best I have ever found."
P.B.*, Bellevue, Washington

"I enjoy them more and more
with each passing year."
J.L., Spurlockville, West Virginia

"No matter how full and happy life might be,
it is an enchantment to sit
and read your novels."
D.K., Willowdale, Ontario

"I firmly believe that Harlequin Romances
are perfect for anyone who wants to read
a good romance."
C.R., Akron, Ohio

*Names available on request

Bound for Marandoo

by

KERRY ALLYNE

Harlequin Books

TORONTO • LONDON • NEW YORK • AMSTERDAM • SYDNEY

Original hardcover edition published in 1977
by Mills & Boon Limited

ISBN 0-373-02094-5

Harlequin edition published August 1977

Printed in Canada

CHAPTER ONE

As they drew nearer to the Queensland border Jade Pascoe's anticipation grew, and for the hundredth time that afternoon she swept an impatient hand across her forehead, allowing the slight breeze that was being forced in through the camper-van's windows to cool her damp skin. Helen Nye took her velvet brown eyes from the road for a moment to flash her companion a quick smile.

'We'll soon be in Wayamba,' she said. 'The last signpost only showed another twenty kilometres, so it shouldn't be long now.'

'Thank the Lord for that!' breathed Jade with a heartfelt sigh as she eased herself forward in the seat and pulled at her shirt where it was sticking to the middle of her back with perspiration. 'I'm longing for a shower and change of clothing.'

'Me too.' Now it was Helen's turn to twist uncomfortably in her moist clothes. 'But do you think we'll be able to find work in a small town like Wayamba?'

'I hope so, because I'd like to have a look around the place—see if I can find a gravestone—all that sort of thing.'

'Wouldn't that be something if you could?' Helen flicked back the dark silky fringe of her gamin haircut. 'Tell me the story again,' she ordered.

'You already know it,' laughed Jade, her green eyes twinkling.

'But I might have forgotten some of it—you know what I'm like. Now that we're nearly there you'd better refresh my memory.'

Jade bent one leg and rested a bare foot on the seat while

5

clamping her arms around her knee. She'd discarded her sandals some miles back.

'Okay, here goes. Apparently the first member of my family to come to this country came at the expense of the British Government—in other words, he was transported. He was one Richard (alias Red) Pascoe, who had been convicted of petty larceny at the Norfolk Assizes,' a grin came into play, 'for having stolen a loaf of bread, I believe, and for this he got seven years' hard labour. I'm not too sure when he arrived in the colony—somewhere around the eighteen-twenties, I think.'

'Go on,' urged Helen. 'I think it's fascinating.'

'Well, as you're probably aware, when more and more free settlers began arriving in Australia, convicts were assigned to them as servants—at least, the better behaved ones among them were. They received no wages, but their masters were obliged to feed them and provide them with clothes and bedding. Anyway, my ancestor was assigned to one Nathaniel McGrath who, together with his wife and family, and armed with a Land Grant for goodness knows how many acres, set off over the ranges and finally settled themselves down at a place which they named Marandoo.'

'Then what happened?'

'Apparently Red, that was the name he was most commonly known by, because,' she put a hand to her own long burnished mahogany tresses and grinned, 'he had dark red hair, served out his time on the property but decided to stay on with the McGraths as a hired hand. Shortly afterwards he married another of their servants, Jane Palmer, whereupon they had a child in due course—William, my great-great-grandfather.'

'It's all coming back to me now,' interrupted Helen with a comprehending nod. 'But finish it off so I get the whole story right.'

Jade paused for a moment, concentrating and trying hard to remember the exact details she'd been told by her father.

6

'It appears that Red must have been a personable young man, and a bit of a rogue to boot,' she chuckled, 'because it would seem that he made quite a hit with Miss Caroline McGrath, the daughter of the house, and so the story goes, the two of them eloped one night but, unfortunately, as they were crossing the river the wagon overturned and poor old Red was drowned.'

'That's right, I remember it now—or at least that part of it,' Helen admitted with a smile. 'But what did your father say happened to Caroline, and Red's wife and baby?'

'I gather Caroline was rescued safely, but from there on I know nothing more of her. But Jane was dismissed from the McGraths' service and left the property with her son, vowing lifelong vengeance and all that sort of thing.'

'And did she ever extract her revenge, do you know?'

'Not that I know of, but don't forget that this has been handed down over the years by word of mouth, so there's quite possibly a few discrepancies here and there, although I believe the story's basically true.'

Helen was silent for a time, musing over what Jade had just told her, then, 'Hey, I've just thought of something! If Red was already married, what were he and Caroline planning to do—live together? In *those* days?'

Jade shrugged and spread her hands wide. 'Beats me, but there must have been something going on between them, because Dad gave me a medallion a couple of years ago— you know that gold one I sometimes wear?—and you can still read the engraving on the back. It says quite clearly, "*To R.P. from C.M.*". Although why his wife would keep another woman's present to her husband is beyond me.'

'Maybe she intended using it as evidence against the McGraths, or something like that,' suggested Helen helpfully.

'Could be,' concurred Jade, easing her legs straight out in front of her. 'But I don't know how. Still, I don't expect she was a terribly well-educated girl, so maybe she thought

7

it would prove something. Who knows? It all happened so long ago.'

'And now you're going back to the scene of the crime, as it were. I wonder if the McGraths remember the story as well as your family do.'

Jade smiled deprecatingly. 'Probably not. I expect young Caroline forgot all about Red after a couple of months, married another wealthy member of our squatocracy and lived happily ever after. I can't see the affairs of a one-time servant of the McGraths making any lasting impression on *that* family. I mean, they haven't exactly sunk into obscurity, have they? They and their properties are always rating a mention in the newspaper.'

'That's true,' Helen had to agree. 'But they might remember if we did happen to meet one of them and you mentioned the story. They might even have some written records,' she finished hopefully. History had always been a favourite subject with Helen.

With a husky laugh Jade extracted a cigarette from a packet and lit it before replying.

'For a start I doubt very much if we'll even see any of them, let alone meet them. They also might not like it if I did mention it. It wouldn't be every wealthy family who would care for a stranger to suddenly pipe up in their midst, saying, "You don't happen to remember the story of one of your respected ancestresses eloping with an ex-convict, do you?" A *married* ex-convict at that, I might add!'

She joined in Helen's ensuing laughter, picturing the consternation and indignation such a statement could cause within some families. It was funny, to her way of thinking, how some people could be so touchy over incidents concerning their ancestors—especially since there wasn't a thing they could do about it. What was done, was done, and nothing in the world could change it.

'Hey, is that Wayamba I can see down there?' she

8

brought them both back to the present as they topped a small rise and a cluster of buildings could be seen at the bottom of the next valley, drowsing in the late afternoon sunshine while the heat still shimmered above the curving roadway.

'I sure hope so,' breathed Helen thankfully. 'A few more miles in this weather and I think I'll dissolve into a grease-spot on the seat. Even if we hadn't been planning to stop here I think we've done enough driving for today.'

'Hear, hear! Now just let's hope they've got a decent hotel in town. I don't fancy sleeping in the van tonight—I want a nice comfortable bed.'

Presently, as they drew closer, the girls could make out that it wasn't a very big town—quite the opposite, in fact. There was a large iron-roofed hotel with wide shady ver-andahs running the full length of it, the one upstairs sport-ing a lacy wrought-iron railing; a rambling general store which also served as the post office and bank agency; a garage of no certain vintage with two dilapidated pumps standing quietly like sentinels in the slanting rays of the sun; a small café with gingham curtains at the windows and a large community hall still bearing posters advertising the past three months' attractions.

Helen brought the van to a halt outside the hotel and both girls gratefully moved out of the hot confines of the vehicle to stand on the shady verandah surveying the ap-parently deserted town, but still the only living creature in sight was the straggly mongrel twitching in its sleep in the doorway of the store.

Brushing the day's collection of travelling dust from their jeans, they moved on into the hotel's wide foyer, the walls of which were lined with rural scenes of days gone by, while halfway down on the right-hand side, just past the reception desk, there was a wide polished staircase leading to the rooms upstairs. On the left a door was open, but on peering through they could see no one inside the bar-room,

9

its long shining counter and empty stools awaiting occupants at the end of a hot day to order one of the assortment of wines and spirits from the well-stocked glass shelves.

Slowly they moved up to the reception desk, where Helen tentatively gave the small bell a ring which resounded dully in the vacant hallway. A few minutes later a man's head appeared around a door at the end of the passageway beside the stairs and, on seeing them standing by the desk, he opned the door fully and strode quickly towards them, a tall, solidly built individual in his middle forties with friendly blue eyes and fair curly hair.

'Yes, young ladies? What can I do for you?' he asked, taking his place behind the desk.

'We'd like a double room for a couple of nights, please.' It was Jade who answered with a smile.

The man spun a large book round to face them on the counter. 'Sure thing,' he said. 'Just sign the register.' And as Jade bent to fill in the appropriate line he looked at them inquiringly. 'Why would a couple of girls like you be wanting to stay here for a few days? Got friends in the neighbourhood, have you? Or ...' as a thought came to him, 'perhaps you saw the advertisement?'

Jade finished signing her name and handed the pen to Helen. 'What advertisement was that?' she queried.

'The one for home help out at Marandoo. There's an engagement party coming up shortly and the whole area will be overflowing with visitors. Young Barbara's becoming engaged to a big-time business executive from the city.'

Two interested glances were exchanged. 'Home help, you said?' they questioned as one, then Helen continued, 'That's just the sort of thing we're looking for.'

'We're planning on working our way round Australia,' explained Jade in turn. 'Stopping wherever we want, for as long as we like, and doing whatever we take a fancy to. So far, since we left Melbourne four months ago, we've worked as kennel maids in Wangaratta, shop assistants in Canberra

10

and waitresses in Sydney. Now we're ready for another change in occupation,' she grinned.

The big man shook his head wonderingly. 'The things you girls get up to these days beat me.' His blue eyes twinkled. 'What are the men down your way thinking about, letting two nice-looking girls like you escape them?'

Both girls laughed at this unexpected compliment while their friendly host turned and extracted a key from a ring on the wall behind him, then turning back again he twisted the register to face him.

'Pascoe and Nye, eh? My name's Bob McIntyre—Mac to all and sundry round these parts.'

'Helen and Jade,' the latter girl informed him, responding to the man's open geniality.

'Right. Well, here's your key—number eleven—second on the left at the top of the stairs and looking out over the street so you can get the benefit of the verandah. Bathroom's at the end of the hallway.' He peered over the counter inquiringly. 'Now where's your luggage?'

'Outside in the van,' returned Jade.

'If you like to drive it in round the back you can park off the street and I'll carry your cases upstairs.'

'Thanks very much, Mac,' replied Helen promptly, and hurried out to the oven-like vehicle.

Minutes later Mac was preceding them up the stairs, a large suitcase held easily in each hand, while the girls carried a smaller bag apiece. At number eleven Mac unlocked the door and pushed it wide, enabling Jade and Helen to enter the room. It was a large bedroom, fitted with two single beds covered with bright cotton bedspreads, and a wide mosquito net hung aloft over each. The furniture was old but well-kept and the blinds at the windows had been pulled down to keep the sun from the rose-patterned carpet during the day. There were large doors leading on to the shaded verandah and a wide fan in the middle of the ceiling.

11

Once he had set the cases down by the nearest bed Mac immediately had the fan operating and opened the verandah doors wide to permit the entrance of a little refreshing air as the heat began to leave the day.

'If there's anything you want, don't hesitate to give me a yell. Dinner's between six and eight,' were his last words as he passed out into the hall.

Left on their own, Jade and Helen immediately began unpacking and half an hour later had all their necessary belongings put away and their cases stored on the top of the wardrobes.

'I'll toss you for first use of the bathroom,' suggested Helen, taking a coin from her purse.

'Okay,' agreed Jade, and laughed at the dismal look of disappointment on her friend's face when her own choice of 'heads' came up.

With a short cotton housecoat and clean clothes draped over her arm, toilet bag clutched in one hand, Jade took one of the fluffy towels from the back of their bedroom door and headed down the passage. The bathroom was clearly marked, but on entering the room she was hard put not to laugh. The place was enormous and the shower recess, bath and washbasin commandeered so little of the space that the room could quite easily have accommodated a bedroom suite as well. But the shower was extremely welcome and reviving and that was all she cared about.

'Mac brought the paper up with the advertisement in it,' Helen greeted Jade on her return, handing the newspaper across for her friend to read for herself. 'He also said that most of the hands from Marandoo come into town on Saturday nights and that Mike Johnson, the manager, usually comes with them. He suggested we have a word with him if we want to apply for work.'

Jade raised her head from the paper and sat on the edge of one of the beds. 'That's a good idea,' she concurred with

12

a pleased smile, 'and it is Saturday today, isn't it? I've lost track of the days since we've been on the road this week.'

'It most certainly is, and this means we won't have to hang around for long waiting for a couple of jobs to come up.'

'If the McGraths decide to put us on,' pointed out Jade with unaccustomed sobriety.

Helen looked amazed at the thought. 'But why shouldn't they?' she protested. 'We're good honest working girls. Nicely behaved,' a cheeky grin appeared, 'well, most of the time we are. What more could they ask for?'

'But we haven't had any experience at this sort of thing,' countered Jade.

'We hadn't had any experience with any of the other positions we've taken so far either, but that didn't stop us and, even if I say so myself, I think we've been quite successful at whatever we've chosen to do.' She peered closely at Jade, her brown eyes twinkling. 'Not having second thoughts about it now that we're here, are you?'

'Who? Me?' Jade was honestly surprised that Helen should think such a thing. 'No, of course not, it's just that,' she pushed the paper towards Helen, 'it says they want help for two months. Did we really want to stay here that long?' she asked.

Helen was now collecting her own gear ready for a trip to the bathroom, but she paused long enough to shrug carelessly.

'I'm easy,' she said. 'It'll certainly be something completely different from what we had in mind when we set out, but,' she raised her hands expressively, 'that was the whole idea of this trip, wasn't it? To do whatever we fancied and for as long as we wanted? Besides,' she grinned again, 'I'm rather looking forward to seeing how the other half lives. I have the feeling it will be quite an eye-opener.'

'Just what I was thinking myself,' laughed Jade delightedly. 'Okay then, we're agreed—Marandoo, here we come!'

'For better or worse!' chuckled Helen for a parting shot as she hugged the remaining dry towel to her and slipped out of the room.

CHAPTER TWO

Two hours later the girls were ready and dressed for dinner; Jade in a crisp cotton frock printed with exotic giant sunflowers, slim shoulder straps leaving an expanse of smooth honey-toned skin bare, and Helen in icy white polyester patterned with splashy green leaves, the neckline wide and square for coolness.

Together they descended the wide staircase, exchanging smiles at the loud talking and laughing that now issued from the apparently well-patronised bar-room. Turning right at the bottom of the stairs they found the entrance to the dining room a little further along the passage, and upon their walking into the room a fair-haired teenager came hurrying away from a table on the far side of the room where she had been talking to two men, a wide friendly smile on her face.

'Hi there—I'm Diana McIntyre,' she told them. 'Dad said we had two more guests, so I reserved one of the tables by the windows for you. It's cooler on that side of the room and you can see what's going on in the street too,' she pulled a laughing grimace, '... if anything!'

Jade and Helen returned her smile, introducing themselves while Diana led them to a small white-clothed table by an open window. They noted with pleasure that it definitely wasn't quite so hot on that side of the room.

'I'm afraid I can't stop and talk too long,' said Diana sorrowfully, obviously disappointed at not being able to glean whatever information she could from the town's two most recent visitors, 'but we're always flat out on Saturday nights and very shortly they'll arrive in their droves from the bar.' She leant across the table and picked up the menu which she handed to Jade. 'Now, what would you like?' she asked.

Having given their orders and seen Diana scurrying back to the kitchen as quickly as she was able in her cork-heeled clogs, Jade and Helen turned their attention to the other diners in the room. The two men Diana had been conversing with when the girls first entered were now busily engaged in a discussion of their own. They were dressed similarly in dark pants, white shirts with their sleeves rolled past their elbows and loosened ties in recognition of the weather, and the girls agreed on their occupations as commercial travellers. Three tables away from these gentlemen sat a young couple with two children—visitors passing through, it was decided. Further along on the same side as the girls there was a very young pair—the boy no more than eighteen, the girl sixteen—holding hands surreptitiously under the table and bringing smiles to the lips of the two older girls. The local love-match?

No sooner had Diana come rushing back with their meals than the sound of heavy-shod feet rolled across the polished flooring as the droves of men—young and old—that she had mentioned began swelling the ranks of the diners. In no time at all it seemed that every available seat had been taken.

Covertly Jade looked round the room and tried to appear as though she was concentrating on her meal at the same time. The newcomers were a varied assortment; tall and short, thin and fat, light hair, dark hair, even a redhead among them, but they were all alike in the conformity of their dress—be it drills, moleskins or jeans—and the almost uniform look of sun-bronzed faces and arms that told of a life spent mostly in the great outdoors. There was something about them that immediately singled them out from the city-dweller. Perhaps it was the underlying fact that they led active, vigorous lives—in and out of the saddle—working with animals—but whatever it was, there was an

16

aura about them that wasn't present in a room full of office workers.

It wasn't until Diana came back and hurriedly took their orders for dessert and laughingly whispered, 'You two are causing quite a stir with the rest of our customers, you know,' that Jade realised that Helen and herself were being just as quietly and thoroughly—but in some instances quite openly—appraised in their turn. It was an amusing thought and the pair of them hid their smiles with difficulty. It hadn't occurred to them before but, no doubt, two unescorted young women in town would cause some blatant speculation. The fact that they were two very attractive females as well hadn't entered their heads.

Diana's dextrous handling of plates piled high with steak or roast beef and vegetables had Jade filled with admiration. Their work as waitresses had been nothing compared to what that young girl was managing tonight, and with all the aplomb of one many times her age as she parried the laughing remarks and comments of the men seated at the tables on her trips to and from the kitchen.

During a lull in the frenzy of ordering food, Diana made it back to Jade and Helen's table with two cups of freshly brewed coffee. Putting them down on the table, she took a look through the window into the street.

'I wish that sister of mine would hurry up, she's supposed to be in here helping me tonight. She should have finished at the hall by now.' The engaging smile that followed, showing attractively uneven white teeth, took in both girls seated at the table. 'There's a dance on tonight over at the hall—why don't you come? I can guarantee you'll have a good time.'

Jade and Helen looked at one another. It would be a good chance to meet other people in the district, but neither girl was keen to be the first to set foot in a gathering of complete strangers.

As if sensing their hesitation Diana now offered, 'You

17

can come with my boy-friend, Kenny, and me if you like. That's him over there,' and she pointed out a slightly-built, pleasant-faced boy who was immediately suffused with colour when he became aware of being the object of their discussion and hurriedly lowered his head. 'We'll introduce you around,' Diana concluded her proposition.

'That's very nice of you, Diana. We'd like to come,' Helen replied for both of them, as a deep voice called for the younger girl's attention from across the room.

A cheerful grin acknowledged her summons, but before leaving she informed them with a rush, 'The only trouble is, I don't get off from here until about nine. Is that too late for you?'

'No, that'll be fine. We'll wait for you in the lounge.'

Another grin and Diana was on her way again while the two at the table lit cigarettes and sat back contentedly to enjoy their cups of steaming coffee.

The next moment they noticed Mac make his way into the crowded room and head for a table surrounded by six husky specimens of manhood. Bending low he began talking to a light-haired man of some thirty years with a ruggedly attractive face, wearing a pale blue short-sleeved shirt opened at the neck and cream drill trousers. He looked once towards the girls and then back to Mac, nodding his head thoughtfully before grinning at some remark made by another of his table companions and rising to his feet. Two cigarettes were stubbed out as one when he started walking with a slow easy stride towards the girls' table.

'I'm Mike Johnson,' he told them with a smile as he came to a halt beside the table. 'Manager out at Marandoo. I understand from Mac that you're interested in the positions we advertised.'

Both girls nodded. 'Yes, we are interested, Mr Johnson,' affirmed Jade.

He looked about him for an empty chair but on finding none suggested, 'If you've finished your coffee it might be

18

better if we headed for the lounge. We can talk in there ... and,' he gave them a wry smile, 'you'd better make it Mike, we very rarely use surnames out here.'

Nodding compliance, Jade and Helen followed him from the dining room amid calls of, 'Don't be greedy, Mike, introduce the rest of us,' and, 'You can't keep both of them for yourself, Mike,' which he waved aside with a tolerant grin. In the lounge and seated on a comfortably upholstered brown leather sofa he apologised ruefully.

'Sorry about that, but with the shortage of good-looking young females out here, you can't really blame them.'

'Don't worry about it,' urged Jade with an infectious laugh. 'After all, I suppose you could say it was a compliment—at least they considered us worthy of an introduction.'

'They would that,' Mike gave credit in his own quiet way before sorting out which girl was which and getting down to business. 'Firstly, we wanted someone who could act as Sarah's companion—that's the boss's grandmother—and do some secretarial work. Gwen Kearney, the wife of one of the hands, was doing it, but she's having a baby shortly and she's finding it too much for her, especially with the heat of summer coming on.'

'Secretarial work would be in Jade's line,' broke in Helen. 'I'm hopeless on a typewriter. What does the other position entail?'

'That's more in the nature of an assistant for the house-keeper, Jenny. It would involve general helping in the house and the kitchen, that kind of thing. Although,' his glance took in both girls, 'in either position you're likely to be called upon to assist in whatever function is most necessary. At a time like this we all turn our hand to anything that's required.'

'Suits me,' agreed Jade easily. 'What about you, Helen?'

'I don't mind, and I rather think I'd prefer the second job—I like cooking and messing around in the kitchen.'

'Good—that's settled then.' Mike was obviously pleased at the outcome. 'But,' his tone sounded a warning, 'you'll have to see the boss in the morning to get a final okay— although I can't see any problems there,' he finished on a more promising note. 'If he puts in an appearance here tonight I'll see about fixing up a time for your appointment.'

It was just as well their discussion was completed, for now the hearty diners began straggling out of the dining room and, while the older members of their company headed straight back to the bar, the younger ones made their presence felt in the lounge. Soon the trio on the sofa were surrounded by smiling exuberant males, all requesting introductions. These completed, Jade and Helen were left with only a vague notion as to whose name belonged to whom and that the stocky dark-haired man was Peter, the tall thin one was Frank, while the nice-looking young lad in the lemon shirt was Eric what's-his-name?

Mac came in carrying a tray filled with overflowing glasses and the girls each found herself being handed a long cool lager and lime, together with the observation that beer was better for you than spirits in a hot climate because it was a longer and more refreshing drink, although watching Peter drain his tall glass Jade decided that a single nip of whisky couldn't possibly have disappeared any faster than that fifteen ounces of good draught.

Questions as to where the girls had come from, what they did for a living, how long they planned to stay, and many others cut across the general talk and laughter. After a long week filled with hard work on the nearby properties it was evident that these young men thoroughly enjoyed their Saturday evenings in town and the chance afforded them to let off steam.,

The young man perched on the arm of the sofa next to Jade—she thought she could remember Mike calling him

20

Gary—paid Mac for another round of drinks and leant forward conspiratorially.

'Come on now, you two, tell us the truth,' he invited with laughing brown eyes and an engaging grin, obviously making fun of what he was about to say. 'Why did you come all the way out here? Was it to find husbands to keep you in the manner to which you're accustomed?'

It was Jade who answered in kind. 'Oh, no!' she laughed up at him. 'I'm looking for a husband who can afford to keep me in a manner to which I'm *un*accustomed!'

Amid the laughter that followed Jade chanced to look past Gary and caught sight of a man standing by the doorway on the fringe of the crowd. A man she hadn't seen before—she would have remembered him if she had! Quite the most startlingly handsome one she had ever seen; broad-shouldered and muscular, dressed in a pale fawn bush shirt and matching drill pants which were belted to slim hips. Dark tousled hair fell forward slightly on to a broad forehead above dark faintly arched brows, beneath which a pair of slate-grey eyes coldly and contemptuously raked her from head to foot. She caught her breath involuntarily and turned her head away with only a hint of the straight nose, curving mouth and strong determined jaw registering an impression on her mind.

Who was he? He looked no different by way of his dress from any other man in the room. Admittedly there had been an unmistakable air of authority about him—but then Mike had that same air about him also to some degree. More importantly, why should he have been looking at her in such a contemptuous manner?

Jade racked her brains searching for an answer and in her quest she glanced again towards the open door, but no help was forthcoming there, for the man in question had disappeared. With a sigh she gave up. What did it matter? She would probably never come across him again—no

21

doubt he was only the manager of some other station in the area.

She searched in her bag for a cigarette and had three lighters flickering under her nose before she could find her own. This small act restored her equilibrium somewhat and she smiled her thanks at Gary when she accepted his light. A second lager and lime was placed on the small table in front of her and, forcing that strange encounter to the back of her mind, Jade again entered into the joking conversation milling around her.

At nine o'clock sharp Diana McIntyre, her bashful boyfriend lagging discreetly at a distance, pushed through the crowd until she was within speaking distance of the two girls on the sofa.

'We were just on our way over to the dance,' she told them. 'Do you still want to come?'

'Too right we're coming to the dance,' Gary answered for them with a broad smile, and drained the remains of his glass in one go. 'Ready, girls?'

Jade and Helen nodded their assent and with Gary linking a brown arm with Jade, and Mike doing the same with Helen, the foursome led the way from the lounge with the rest of the assembly following in groups of twos and threes out into the cool night air, which Jade drank in deeply after the smoke-filled environs of the hotel, and across the street into the brightly lit and gaily decorated community hall.

There was a resounding dance already in progress, and before Jade had time to assimilate her surroundings Gary had whirled her into the crowded press of dancers already occupying the floor. A quick look over her shoulder showed that Helen and Mike were just disappearing into the swarm at the other end of the building. Gary was a good dancer and Jade found her steps matching his effortlessly.

Turning her bright head, she looked to the teak-brown face above her. 'Do you work at Marandoo as well, Gary?'

Brown eyes surveyed the lovely features in front of him

appreciatively. 'Sure do,' he replied with his customary grin. 'I'm a senior jackeroo—in my third year now—employed by the McGrath Pastoral Company. I've done a year in the Riverina district, a year down on the south coast and now almost a year up here.'

'I didn't know they moved jackeroos around like that. I thought you just stayed put on the one property.'

'Uh-huh!' he shook his head decisively. 'Quite a few of the large pastoral companies move their trainees around so that they get a good grounding in all facets of station management and know-how. We're also sent to college, which means there's exams and all, you know,' he added regretfully.

'And what happens when you've completed your courses and passed all your exams?'

'Usually you do a stint in the company's city offices,' drily.

'Whatever for?'

His brows rose humorously. 'Who questions the powers-that-be?' he laughed. 'But, seriously, it's so that you're prepared, if called upon, to take over any suitable position vacant within the company. That's why we're shifted from property to property. It's no use if you've done your whole time on a property up north and then you're sent to take charge in the south of the State. The soil, weather conditions, everything is completely different. You've got to have some knowledge of the area in which you're placed to be able to do the best for the company.'

'I had no idea there was so much to it,' commented Jade in surprise.

'Most city people haven't,' he agreed laconically.

A thunderous crescendo on the drums denoted the end of that particular dance and Gary led Jade back through the chattering throng to the seats lining the walls. Shortly Helen and Mike joined them, as well as a number of their companions from the hotel. Jade was amazed at the amount of unattached males present, but supposed that would nearly always be the case in small towns such as Wayamba where there were a lot of large properties catering for a high male employee rate but a very small female one.

From then on neither Jade nor Helen had time to catch breath after one dance before being claimed for the next. It was an exhilarating experience and one guaranteed to raise any girl's morale at least ten points. But it was also hard on the feet, and by the time a halt was called for supper both of them were thankful for the chance to sit down for a few minutes.

Still hovering protectively—or was it possessively?—around them, Mike scrutinised the legion in the supper room and turned to Gary.

'Have you seen the boss anywhere around tonight? I wanted to make arrangements for Helen and Jade to see him tomorrow.'

Gary finished the last mouthful of a slice of luscious fruit cake and also scanned the scores of heads.

'Saw him earlier in the evening, but not since coming over to the hall,' he told Mike.

'Oh, I thought I caught sight of him a while ago,' Mike explained, 'but I must've been mistaken.'

'You'd know if he was here all right,' returned Gary eyeing Mike with a knowing grin. 'Miss Laura Emery would see to that.'

Mike looked doubtful as to whether he should agree with Gary or not and ended up by smiling faintly, reprovingly, and shaking his head.

'It's no business of ours, Gary, how the boss's girl-friend behaves.'

'But I'm entitled to my opinion,' countered Gary irrepressibly.

Jade and Helen looked up at the two of them with interest. 'Isn't Mr McGrath married?' queried a surprised Helen.

24

'Who? Tory?' Gary laughed at the expression on her face. 'No fear! Should he be?'

'Well, I...' Helen was flustered and not quite sure what to say, so Jade interpreted with a grin, 'It's just that we pictured him as a middle-aged man tending to corpulence with a large brood of children.'

At this both Mike and Gary couldn't restrain their laughter and it was some time before Mike could manage, 'Oh, that's a good one. We'll have to let Tory in on it the next time we see him.'

'Don't you dare!' two voices ordered together. 'Perhaps you'd better just tell us what he *is* like, so we don't go making any more mistakes,' suggested Helen hopefully.

'Well ... he's thirty-six years old, tall...' Mike scratched at his head perplexedly. 'What else can I tell you? He's a man's man, but I'd guess you'd say he was a woman's man at the same time. He's got a girl-friend, Laura Emery, who lives some twenty miles distant—sorry, thirty-two kilometres—on the other side of town...' A, 'Thank God for that!' was interspersed here by a laughing Gary, which earned him another warning look from Mike. '... He has a younger brother, Reid, who's married and lives in Brisbane with his family, and a younger sister, Barbara, whose engagement party we're needing the help for. His parents are dead—killed in a plane crash about ten years ago—and his grandmother, old Sarah McGrath, still lives on the property.'

'And what's his grandmother like? Perhaps I should know something about her too if I'm going to apply for the post of her companion.'

Here Gary took up the role of informer. 'Sarah's a real sweetie by anyone's standards. She's almost eighty but doesn't look a day over seventy, although her arthritis has curtailed her activities a lot over the past year or so. She likes people with "spirit" as she calls it, and doesn't believe in mincing words herself either!' He gave an emphatic nod.

'A trait her grandson has inherited to the full! But if you ever need a friend, or a word of advice, then Sarah's the one to turn to—she's a wise little lady, that one!'

Jade digested this in thoughtful silence, not certain whether she was attempting to become the companion of a fire-eating dragon of a pioneer woman, or of a sweet old lady with a heart of gold. Oh, well, time would tell. It was only for a couple of months after all.

The raucous beat of the band reverberated through the building once more, signalling that the dancing was about to begin again, and Jade and Helen were swiftly whisked on to the crowded floor. By the time midnight arrived both girls were feeling the effects of a long day spent travelling in the hot van, combined with more exercise than they had taken for the past six months, and it was with considerable relief that they finally heard the musicians strike their last note, allowing Gary and Mike to escort them back to the hotel.

At the foot of the stairs Helen turned back to Mike. 'What time should we come out in the morning? Or do you think it would be better if we rang first?'

'No need,' smiled Mike confidently. 'Make it around nine. If Tory's not there you can have a look around the place and have a word with Sarah instead. Once she approves of you you're more than halfway there.'

With casual salutes the two men strode for the door with easy swinging steps while Jade and Helen made their way more slowly, and a lot less vigorously, up the staircase and along to their room. Inside, with one accord, both girls threw themselves full-length on their respective beds, kicking off their shoes and wriggling their feet ecstatically in the freedom which ensued.

'You know what?' laughed Jade suddenly, propping herself up on one elbow to face her friend. 'We forgot to ask them how to get there.'

Helen clapped a hand to her mouth in dismay. 'Whatever

26

will we...?' then she too laughed and relaxed. 'I doubt if even we could miss a property the size of Marandoo. How many acres is it?'

'Quite some thousands, I believe. I don't know exactly,' yawned Jade.

For a few minutes there was absolute silence in the room, then Helen sat up with a start.

'If I'm not careful I'll go to sleep dressed just as I am. I'm off to the bathroom for a wash ... coming?'

Jade nodded drowsily and slid reluctantly off the bed, picking up her toiletries on the way to the door. Together they padded their way to the bathroom and Jade sat on the edge of the bath while Helen cleaned her teeth and washed her face. It was while Jade was at the washbasin that Helen brought the subject up.

'What did you think of Mike?' she asked tentatively— too tentatively—causing Jade to flick her an interrogating glance.

'Nice,' replied Jade non-committally, wondering what was coming next.

'I liked him,' Helen confessed softly, then more surely, 'I liked him a lot.'

Now that she could see the turn the conversation was taking Jade smiled through the soap bubbles covering her face.

'I thought you did,' she remarked impishly, splashing icy cold water over her skin and grabbing for her towel.

'Was I that obvious?' Helen now asked in dismay.

'Only to me,' Jade relieved her friend's mind. 'I've known you too long not to recognise the signs, and he's your type down to the ground.'

'Oh!' Helen seemed surprised. 'Do I have a particular type? I haven't noticed.'

Collecting her things, Jade led the way back to the bedroom.

'You certainly do,' she told Helen surely. 'The strong

quiet type who measure up their words before they speak. Extremely dependable, one and all!'

'There's nothing wrong with being dependable,' Helen immediately came to Mike's defence. 'I should think that would be a characteristic every woman would look for in the man she proposed to marry.'

'Talking about marriage now, are we?' teased Jade. 'My, my, you have got it bad, haven't you?'

Helen flushed self-consciously.

'You know I didn't mean it that way. I only meant it as a generalisation—I wasn't particularly referring to Mike.'

'I know, I know,' Jade took pity on her with a smile. 'I like the dependable ones too, you know where you are with them.'

In a trice the girls were donning shortie pyjamas and pulling back the coverings on their beds, but before clambering in Jade ambled over to the doors leading on to the verandah.

'Shall we leave these open?' she asked indifferently.

'It'll be an invitation to every mosquito and moth within a ten-mile radius,' Helen warned sleepily.

Jade glanced towards the ceiling and smiled wryly.

'I rather think half the colony came without an invitation anyway,' she commented on seeing the little black insects clinging to the paintwork, and pushed the glass doors wider with a shrug. When they already had so many, what did a few more matter?

Quickly she turned the light out by the door and scrambled on to her bed and under the netting, listening to the immediate droning as the annoying pests dive-bombed the protective coverings in an effort to reach the girls' supine bodies. Jade smiled into the darkness as the attacks were foiled again and again, and rolling on to her side she murmured a tired 'G'night,' to Helen and received an even sleepier response before sliding into a deep welcome unconsciousness.

CHAPTER THREE

A HEFTY banging on the door heralded the arrival of Diana the next morning with two cups of tea and a plate of plain biscuits which she placed on the table beside Jade's bed.

'If you'd like to tell me now what you want for breakfast, I can have it ready for you when you come down,' she offered.

Jade pushed herself up, struggled out from beneath the mosquito netting and picked up one of the cups, sipping the hot brew carefully.

'Thanks, Diana, but I'll just have coffee and toast. What about you, Helen?' as the other girl also came to sit on the edge of the bed to drink her tea.

'The same for me too,' was her reply between mouthfuls of the scalding drink.

'Gee, you're easy pleased. Are you sure that's all you want? Don't you have cereal, or anything like that?' Clearly Diana was used to big appetites.

Jade and Helen smiled, shaking their heads.

'No, neither of us cares much for eating early in the morning,' explained Helen cheerfully.

Diana plumped herself down on the end of the bed, clearly disposed to enjoy a cosy chat.

'What did you think of the dance last night? Did you have a good time?' she wanted to know.

'Very good, thank you. Did you?' inquired Jade politely.

This was evidently the opening Diana had been waiting for, because she immediately became all dreamy-eyed.

'Oh, yes, I had a marvellous time,' she enthused. 'And Kenny said he thought it was the best one we'd been to.'

She fixed the girls with an interested look. 'What did you think of Kenny? Isn't he sweet? He said he thought I was the best looking girl there ... I know I wasn't, of course ... but wasn't it nice of him to say that?'

There appeared to be only one reply that could be made to such a question and that was to agree, which both girls did, accompanied by what they both hoped were suitable expressions of effusiveness.

'*Diana!*'

A roar came from the bottom of the stairs, making the younger girl jump guiltily.

'Ooh, that's Dad,' she explained unnecessarily. 'I'd better be on my way.' At the door she turned back. 'I'll see you later and we can talk some more then,' she told them in her most confidential manner.

'Oh, no, I couldn't bear it,' laughed Helen once the door had closed. 'Not if it means we're going to have to hear every solitary thing that Kenny said, did, or thought.' She sobered quickly. 'Were we ever as bad as that?'

'I hope not,' returned Jade with feeling, and grinned. 'But we could have been without realising it. I expect Diana will outgrow it in time like the rest of us.'

'Umm, I expect so.' Helen now had other things on her mind as she sorted through her clothes in the wardrobe. 'What are you going to wear today, Jade?'

'Slacks, most probably. Why?'

'I wondered whether we should wear dresses. You know, create a good impression and all that.'

Jade shrugged nonchalantly. 'Start as you mean to go on, Dad always says. Besides, I own more slacks than I do dresses, and if they don't like them it's better to find out before we start working there than afterwards. Why, you don't think they're planning to dress us up in little black dresses with frilly white aprons and mob caps, do you?' she laughed gleefully.

'Wouldn't that be something to see?' Helen grinned, seeing the funny side of it.

In the end they both decided on slacks; Jade in white denims with navy blue scroll-work embroidered halfway up the sides and a navy blue and white top that curved to her figure lovingly; Helen in pale orange slacks with a matching orange and green patterned top that set off her creamy olive complexion outstandingly.

A quick breakfast in the dining room, followed by instructions from Mac on how to get there, and Jade and Helen were soon out in the van and happily bound for Marandoo. The already burning sun was still climbing inexorably towards its zenith in the clear blue sky, but the air blowing into the vehicle and making the girls' hair fly jauntily was still clear and fresh to the skin.

The grass in the paddocks was green, but the leaves on the trees hung limp and dusty, patiently awaiting the next fall of rain. The peacefully grazing cattle looked well fed and well cared for, judging by the lustrous shine on their hides, and now and again colourful birds swooped and darted as they winged their chattering way over the landscape. All was serene and contented and, exchanging quick glances, Jade and Helen smiled—it was a good time of the day to be out on the road.

As Mac had correctly foretold, it was impossible to miss the turning into the property, and after rattling over the first cattle grid the girls looked about them with interest. The scenery here was a mixture of cleared paddocks and densely wooded hills, but as the narrow road wound its way alongside the first of the steep inclines they could see a gap in the ridges ahead and, once having passed through it, they came upon the rolling grasslands that stretched as far as they could see into the distance, with only clumps and stands of trees here and there to emphasise the splendour of the panorama. Away on the left they thought they could make out what could be the homestead and outbuildings glinting in the early morning sunshine, together with the unmistakable gleam and shimmer of water nearby.

Jade eased her foot from the accelerator and began the slow descent past numerous neatly symmetrical paddocks, herds of quietly grazing cattle, over more grids and through wide unwieldy steel gates until, at last, the final one was behind them and they were travelling on the neatly laid driveway towards the homestead. But what a homestead! It took Jade's breath away, even though she was sure she'd seen a photograph of it somewhere before—in a magazine probably—but now, seeing it in real life, she realised that the picture couldn't possibly have done full justice to it.

The first thing that struck her was the sheer beauty of the magnificent warm-tinted sandstone building. The wide slate-paved verandahs and delicately traced iron balconies with their connecting fluted pillars all combined to give it an air of graciousness and space amidst its setting of wide green lawns surrounded by stately gums and casuarinas, while the mullioned windows blinked back the sunlight with gleaming sparkles.

No sooner had the van pulled to a halt beside the front porch than Mike came striding round one corner of the building. He had evidently been keeping a watch for their arrival and smiled at Helen when she alighted. A smile which was returned eagerly by the recipient, noted Jade with some amusement.

'Tory didn't seem keen on having any interviews today,' Mike apologised with a perplexed crease furrowing across his brow, 'which I can't understand because I would have thought he'd have been only too pleased at having the chance to fill the positions so quickly. Anyway,' his tone lightened with pleasure, 'Sarah has been anxiously awaiting your arrival.' He grinned, his blue eyes twinkling attractively. 'Says she's interested to see these two girls who go gallivanting—her word, not mine—around the countryside unescorted. Now, would you like to meet Sarah first, or see over the place a bit beforehand?'

It was Jade who answered. 'No, let's get the meeting over and done with first. Who knows?' she shrugged fatalistically, 'once the interview's over there may be no need for us to stay and have a look around.'

'You're not usually such a defeatist, Jade,' exclaimed Helen in a shocked voice. 'Have you changed your mind about applying for work?'

'No, I haven't changed *my* mind, but it sounds as if Mike's boss might have done. Surely, if his is the final say-so, and he isn't here to say one way or the other, then it was a waste of our time coming.'

'You're wrong there,' broke in Mike, pleased to be able to offer some encouragement. 'If Sarah takes to you, she can hire you on the spot if she chooses. Make a good impression on her and she'll fight Tory tooth and nail to keep you.'

'But does she ever *win* in these fights?' queried Jade with a laugh.

'Sure she does,' Mike hastened to assure her, laughing too. 'Tory's pretty tolerant when it comes down to what Sarah really wants.'

'Okay, you win, lead on, Mike. Let's see just what Sarah McGrath does make of two girls who go *gallivanting* around the country unescorted.'

Past the solid oak main entrance doors they moved into a beautifully panelled foyer, complete with an intricately carved ceiling. In the middle of the parquet flooring stood an obviously antique gate-legged table upon which there reposed a large copper urn filled with variegated coloured chrysanthemums. At the back of this there was a wide staircase leading to the upper storey and from the sides there were many sets of doors leading to other rooms, one of which Mike led them to.

A faint, 'Come in,' was the response to his knocking on what he informed them was the library door, and upon entering the room Jade's first brief impression was one of light perspective as she quickly scanned the shelves of books that rose to the ceiling on right and left of her; the wide open doors that led on to the slate verandah, cool and shady; the enormous slate fireplace that dominated the fourth wall, before her gaze came to rest on the little white-haired lady seated in a deeply padded white leather arm-chair placed to one side of the hearth.

As Gary had said, Sarah McGrath didn't look her eighty years; her skin was still soft and to a great extent un-wrinkled, her periwinkle blue eyes had lost none of their brilliance. From their astute gaze it was evident that her brain had lost little of its sharpness either. Deterioration showed only in her hands, which lay bony and gnarled, one on each arm of her chair, as an indication of the arthritic condition which afflicted her physical being but had been unable to subdue her indomitable spirit.

'You can go, Mike,' she waved him away with a slight movement of her right hand. 'I'll have Jenny give you a call if I need you.'

'Okay, Sarah,' Mike acquiesced easily as, with a reassur-ing wink in the girls' direction, he left the room.

'Well now,' Sarah seemed faintly pleased with herself. 'Sit down over there where I can see you,' she ordered, indicating the matching leather sofa opposite her own chair. 'It's Jade and Helen, isn't it?' And after the girls had given affirmative nods, 'Well, which one's which?' she demanded in staccato tones.

This sorted out, Sarah turned her attention to Helen, asking what she did for a living, and on being told that Helen was, by profession, a kindergarten teacher, pursed her lips thoughtfully and murmured, 'That could be help-ful.'

The questions kept coming, some of them seeming to be idly inconsequential, others shrewd and pointed, and as she apparently wasn't to be included in this portion of the interview Jade allowed her glance to wander.

There was a lovely old-fashioned writing desk with an accompanying straight-backed chair that she had missed on her first inspection because it was towards the corner of the room and had been partially hidden by the opened door, and she hated to think what that blue and gold carpet beneath her feet had cost, because it was absurdly soft and luxuriously deep. Her glance roamed back to the bookshelves—everyone of them full with handsome leather-bound editions. She could guess that some of them must have been extremely old and some had been handled far more often than others.

She came back to the present with a start, aware that Helen had risen from her seat and was disappearing through the doors on to the verandah, and that Sarah had spoken her name.

'I said—are you interested in books?' Sarah repeated her question sharply.

Jade brought her eyes back to the woman in front of her.

'I'm—I'm sorry,' she apologised, a soft rosy blush staining her cheeks under Sarah's piercing look. 'Yes, I like them very much—I enjoy reading.'

Was that a slight softening in Sarah's eyes she could see? Jade hoped so—she hadn't made a very auspicious start!

'And what is *your* occupation?'

'I'm a secretary.'

'Is that all?'

Jade's brows rose slightly. Wasn't that enough?

'I have done some part-time television modelling,' she offered confusedly, not quite certain what information it was that Sarah wanted.

A satisfied nod greeted this remark. 'I thought I'd seen your face somewhere. It's not one people would forget in a hurry.'

35

Was that good or bad? mused Jade wryly. With Sarah you couldn't tell.

'And you want to be my companion, is that right?'

'That's correct, Mrs McGrath.' Jade was on surer ground now.

'Why?' barked Sarah suddenly.

The firm ground was just as quickly swept out from under Jade's feet and she sought frantically for an answer that would satisfy the woman in front of her. When nothing suitable came to mind she gave up, smiled, and told the truth.

'Because we wanted to stay around this area for a while and that position happened to be advertised.' Now she was sure a verbal blast would be forthcoming.

But it wasn't. Instead Sarah began to show signs of humour.

'At least you're honest,' she approved. 'And you've got a pretty smile,' albeit this appeared to be admitted grudgingly, 'for I can't stand sour faces around me. You'll be expected to lend a hand wherever extra help is needed. You needn't think this is going to be an easy post, full of free time.'

Jade gave a denying shake of her head. 'I didn't expect it to be, Mrs McGrath. And the idea of giving a helping hand doesn't worry me—that was partly the reason Helen and I began this trip, so we could try out a variety of work.'

For some reason Sarah appeared to be trying to discourage her from the position and Jade couldn't understand why. There was a definite puzzle here and she wondered how long it would be—if ever—before it unravelled and revealed itself.

'All right then,' Sarah made up her mind swiftly. 'I'll give you a try. When do you want to start? Tomorrow morning? . . . the same as your friend?'

Jade was surprised. She hadn't realised that Helen had been definitely engaged, but then perhaps that wasn't so amazing after all, she hadn't been paying much attention to the previous interview. Now she replied quickly.

'Yes, that'll be fine, Mrs McGrath. What time would suit you best?'

'Nine o'clock—the same as today.' Sarah's eyes ranged over Jade appraisingly, then she pointed to her slacks. 'Are they what you wear all the time?'

So the crunch was yet to come! Had Helen been right after all in suggesting they should have worn dresses? Well, she would soon see.

'They're what I have most of,' she answered truthfully.

'No doubt,' snorted Sarah disparagingly. 'You show most of what you've got in those things too!'

A husky laugh escaped Jade before she could stop it. 'You could be right, but that isn't the reason I wear them. It's because they're comfortable and easy to launder.'

'So my granddaughter, Barbara, keeps telling me,' a faint chuckle issued from Sarah's disapproving lips. 'But I don't believe her either!'

Feeling that the interview was at an end, Jade rose quickly to her feet and moved towards the door, but Sarah hadn't finished yet.

'You'll still have to see my grandson, Tory, before you leave. He's the one who sets the wages and deals with that side of the business. It's not usual for me to employ the staff, but I thought, in the circumstances, I might take a hand this time.' She motioned towards the verandah doors. 'You can go out that way. No doubt Mike Johnson and your friend will be hovering close to hand.'

Thanking her, Jade made her exit as rapidly as possible, crossed the paved walk and began moving slowly down the steps on to the close-cropped lawn. She looked back once over her shoulder and shook her head wonderingly. She wasn't at all confident she was doing the right thing in accepting the position. Sarah McGrath hadn't come across quite as Mike and Gary had described her. To Jade's mind

37

she seemed a rather autocratic and irascible old lady who would take very careful handling if Jade wasn't to jeopardise her position every time they met.

'How did it go? Did you get the job?' asked Helen excitedly, making Jade jump because she hadn't seen her and Mike approaching.

Jade nodded slowly. 'I guess so, although she said I still have to see her grandson before we leave.'

'That's what she said to me too,' chattered Helen, casting a happy look at Mike, only to find him studying her friend closely.

'What's up, Jade?' he inquired. 'Don't you like the sound of it?'

'Oh, no, nothing like that,' she evaded quickly, flashing them a brilliant smile. She didn't want to spoil Helen's pleasure in being able to work in close proximity to Mike. 'It's just that...' she wrinkled her nose musingly, 'she wasn't quite as I expected. To me she seemed as if she was spoiling for a fight.'

Mike gave a low chuckle. 'In that case, you've got nothing to worry about, because if Sarah wants a fight she'll have it—and no beg pardons asked. So, whoever it is she's wanting to clash with, you can be sure it wasn't you!'

'You mean that under that hard exterior there *does* beat a heart of gold?' Jade laughed flippantly.

'Something like that—but there's no need for you to worry your head over it now. I saw Tory go into the house shortly after you came out, so while he and Sarah have their discussion I'll show you some of the other buildings and then you can both see him when we get back.'

So saying, Mike led the girls across the lawn, past the massive shrubbery and through a small gate set in the side fence and on to the stores building.

Returning from their inspection the best part of an hour later, Mike this time guided Jade and Helen through the house to a small ante-room outside the station office, where he left them seated on a small couch while he entered the inner sanctum. A few minutes later he emerged and beckoned to Helen.

'You're first,' he told her with an encouraging smile and whispered, 'I'll see you tomorrow morning, probably. Good luck!'

Helen passed through into the office and closed the door while Mike came to stand in front of Jade.

'Sorry to have to rush off, Jade, but I'd better get back to work. Good luck to you too,' he bade her, making for the hallway.

On her own, Jade stared about her curiously. At the prettily marked wallpaper, the glorious oil painting of a windjammer under full sail that adorned one wall, the beautiful lace curtains which were tied back on either side of the window near where she was sitting. These drew her attention to the view outside and she found herself looking towards a silver snake of a river that wound its way past a small dilapidated building beneath some tall trees not far from the water's edge. She felt her pulse rate begin to quicken. Could that possibly be the original homestead? It wasn't one of the outbuildings, because Mike had already shown them all of those and they were all on the opposite side of the house. Even from here she could tell that it was very old, and she fell to musing whether that could possibly be where Red had served his time as an assigned servant.

Without warning she looked up to see Helen standing beside her, a thumb and forefinger making a circle of victory as she murmured hastily, 'Go on in, he's waiting for you.' Her eyebrows slanted expressively. 'You'll like him— he's really something!'

The corners of Jade's mouth turned up in amusement. That was some admission from Helen, who had just become so smitten by Mike Johnson. This one she had to see for herself!

39

With a light tread she walked into the office and closed the door behind her, but on encountering the deep grey stony gaze of the man at the desk in front of the window, Jade gave an inward gasp of pure dismay and felt the tell-tale stain of colour rushing to her face as she leant back against the door for support.

This was the same man she had seen the night before in the hotel lounge—and he had been staring at her in the same disparaging manner then—and still Jade could find no valid reason for it. She shook her head disbelievingly and saw a gleam of scorn in his face. He indicated the chair in front of his desk.

'Sit down, Miss Pascoe,' she was ordered in a cold voice. 'I'll be with you in a minute.'

Jade swallowed hard and reluctantly did as she was bid, clenching her hands together apprehensively in her lap while she studied the downbent head. The light from the window played over the side of his face, throwing the strong profile into stark relief against the darker background of office furniture. Even now she knew who he was and what he apparently thought of her personally—although she still couldn't guess the reason why—she unwillingly had to agree with Helen's description, and her own first appraisal—he really was the most magnetic male she had ever seen!

Abruptly he lifted his eyes from the papers before him and caught her scrutiny. Jade held his steely-eyed glance for as long as she could until, catching her bottom lip between her teeth, she fanned dark lashes down and hid her own jewel-bright eyes from view. The man was too arrogant for words, she concluded.

'You must be feeling quite pleased with yourself, Miss Pascoe.' His opening words brought Jade's glance upwards again, away from the pen-stand sitting on the front of the desk which her eyes had been examining so minutely, to stare at him in doubtful confusion. 'Was it very difficult for you to hoodwink my grandmother so successfully?'

Jade's thoughts were floundering in a mire of chaos. Whas was he talking about?

'I—I beg your p-pardon?' she stammered.

'It's a little late for that, Miss Pascoe,' he took her words at face value with a hatefully sarcastic inflection. 'I realise it must have come as something of a shock to you to have your plans revealed to the wrong quarter, but,' his mouth curved into a scornful smile, 'you really shouldn't have been so eager to make them public!'

Plans! What plans? Jade felt as if she were becoming deeper and deeper enmeshed in a web that no one had thought to tell her was there.

'But I haven't any idea what you're talking about!' Her voice rose a little wildly as she fought to impress her ignorance upon the man in front of her.

Tory leant back in his deep chair, completely in control of the situation, whereas Jade sat forward on the edge of her own, nervously clasping and unclasping her fingers, her face burning at his deliberately insolent inspection of her person.

'Oh, no, I'm sure you haven't!' There it was again, that despicable sarcasm. 'But although you may have managed to trick my grandmother with that studied innocence of yours,' there was raw fury in that voice now as he suddenly moved forward and brought a clenched fist down on to the desk top with a heavy thud, 'don't play me for the same kind of fool, Miss Pascoe, because I'm not that gullible!'

Jade jumped back warily, blinking in her agitation. It was patently clear that he was only restraining his temper with difficulty, and it was just as clear in whose direction that fury would be expended should she inadvertently provoke him into losing it. Deciding that silence was her best protection, Jade chewed at her lip apprensively and concentrated once more on the marble pen-stand.

'Well, Miss Pascoe?'

With a gulp and a sharply drawn breath, Jade brought her gaze back to his and courageously stuck to her guns.

'I still haven't the faintest idea what you're talking about, Mr McGrath,' she murmured huskily.

'So we still intend to play innocent, do we?' he remarked with satiric patience, leaning back at ease once again in his chair, but allowing Jade a small sigh of relief for the fact that his anger seemed well under control once more. 'But you needn't think that if you keep up the act long enough I shall believe it, because I can assure you, I shall not! I heard your careless remark in the hotel with my own ears ... remember?'

A frown of deep thought creased Jade's smooth brow as she tried to conjure up the conversation he was referring to. Just before she had noticed him for the first time she had been laughing at Gary—everyone had been laughing—and it had been at something she'd said. Oh, yes, it was coming back to her now, she'd jokingly told them, 'I'm looking for a husband who can afford to keep me in a manner to which I'm *un*accustomed.'

Now that this particular riddle had been solved the frown disappeared from her face and she leant back relaxedly in her own chair, but then she did what was apparently the worst possible thing she could have done—she smiled— a delightful shaping of a soft mouth that brought a laughing twinkle to her green eyes.

At the glacial narrowed-eyed look and the tightening of the shapely mouth of the man across the desk, Jade immediately realised what interpretation had been placed upon that smile and swiftly wiped the expression from her face, sitting forward tensely and saying fervently, 'But that was—was a joke ... a game ...'

'You might consider it a *joke*, or a *game*, Miss Pascoe,' the tones were as stark as ever, 'but let me tell you, I for one don't consider gold-digging little hussies like you a *joke*! Do I make myself clear?'

42

Her reputation in shreds at her feet after one hasty character analysis, Jade felt her own temper beginning to rise and she began breathing deeply, replying in a voice as icy as his own.

'Perfectly clear, Mr McGrath! But, if you would just let me explain . . .'

He made a negligent movement with one long-fingered hand. 'There are no explanations necessary,' he told her with autocratic mockery. 'I heard you make the remark—your pleased look a moment ago confirmed it.'

'But—but . . . I wasn't . . .'

'Miss Pascoe, please don't make it worse by trying to excuse your materialistic personality.' His supercilious gibing grated on Jade's nerves intolerably.

Gold-digging hussy! Materialistic personality! *How dared he!* Jade's eyes sparkled with the light of battle while she fumed inwardly. If it wasn't for Helen having become so besotted with Mike she would have found immense pleasure in telling Mr McGrath exactly what he could do with his job! As it was she couldn't spoil Helen's holiday for her—even if nothing came of her budding romance—and the light died from her eyes, knowing that, no doubt, *he* would again put the wrong construction upon her silent acquiescence.

'That's better,' he sanctioned hatefully. 'As long as we both know where we stand, and you're aware that I will be keeping a close watch on your activities. This is a working cattle station—not a marriage market.'

'Yes, Mr McGrath,' she answered dully.

'I've arranged for your friend to have the room near our housekeeper, Mrs Jennings, and her husband. There is also a spare room next to my grandmother's suite which I think would be best for you to use in the circumstances.'

Jade only nodded. What the circumstances were that he was talking about she didn't know, but she was determined she wasn't going to ask either!

'As my grandmother's companion you will, of course, be expected to take your meals with the rest of the family in the dining room,' he continued, making her eyes flicker with dismay at the thought, 'and I trust you will conduct yourself with all due propriety while you're there.'

At this Jade's eyes blazed green fire. What did he think she was going to do? Eat from her knife? Or did he perhaps expect her to seduce his guests at the dinner table?

'Of course, Mr McGrath. It might be an effort, you understand, but I promise ... I'll try!' she retorted with her own insolent sarcasm.

The grey eyes gleamed intently, warningly, but all he said was, 'Oh, yes, there was one other thing, Miss Pascoe. I have neither the time nor the inclination to be conducting these interviews more often than I have to. In other words, I don't choose to find you deciding in a week or so's time that the chances of success for your little scheme might be better elsewhere, so I'll have your signature on a contract guaranteeing your services to the McGrath Pastoral Company for the next three months, please.'

Three months! That was longer than she and Helen had at first decided to stay in the area, but presumably Helen had already signed a similar document. However, this time Jade wasn't going to let him have everything his own way, and she held his gaze challengingly.

'Provided, of course, the contract works both ways, Mr McGrath,' she stipulated with creditable calm.

'Both ways, Miss Pascoe?'

'That's right ... both ways. I would also like a guarantee that the company won't dispense with my services for the next three months. It's no use to me either, Mr McGrath, having to keep applying for positions after only a week or so's employment,' she used his own words in retaliation.

He gave a short scathing laugh. 'You couldn't expect any employer to agree to terms such as those. You might not be worth employing for three months.'

Jade refused to give ground. 'And you might not be a tolerable employer for three months,' she pointed out sweetly.

From his expression it was clear that no one had disputed his authority in such a manner before, but as he already thought the worst about her, Jade could see no reason why she shouldn't further the issue—she had nothing more to lose!

'I could be guaranteeing employment to a thief, or worse!'

She wasn't sure whether that was supposed to be another indirect attack upon her character or not, but she was prepared to give him the benefit of the doubt.

'In that case, Mr McGrath, I'll settle for a clause giving you the right to dismiss me should I break the law. I think that's fair.'

One dark eyebrow lifted sardonically. 'How very considerate of you!'

A moment later and he had extracted a printed form from the top drawer of his desk and penned some writing and his signature along the bottom of the page in a strong authoritative hand. Passing the paper to Jade, he inquired mockingly, 'That good enough for you, Miss Pascoe?'

Jade applied her own neat signature and allowed herself the satisfaction of a brief smile.

'I think so, Mr McGrath. Just so long as we *both* know where we stand ... as you so rightly said.'

There was no answering smile, as Jade had known there wouldn't be, and for the rest of the interview Tory McGrath spoke with the usual detachment of a personnel officer. Duties, wages and hours were all discussed, but it was with a great feeling of deliverance that Jade found herself outside the office and back in the ante-room again.

Helen rushed up to her, a happy smile on her face. 'Well, how did it go? You were an awfully long time. What did you think of the boss?'

'Oh, great!' Jade agreed hollowly to both questions, and forced a smile on to her features for her friend's benefit. 'Just great!' she repeated slowly.

Together they headed for the hallway looking for the front door, but as they turned out of the room they almost bumped into a small motherly brown-haired little woman coming from the back of the house. She had lively faded blue eyes and rosy cheeks. Her print dress was almost completely enveloped in a large white apron that was tied loosely round the middle of her ample proportions. Recovering from the near collision, the older woman spoke first.

'You must be the Helen and Jade that Mike was telling me about. I'm Mary Jennings, the housekeeper, nicknamed Jenny by everyone this side of Wayamba.' She smiled at the two fresh young faces before her and spoke to the dark-haired girl first. 'You'll be Helen?' and at that girl's eager nod, 'And you'll be working with me?'

'That's right—I've just got the job.'

'Good.' She patted Helen's arm softly. 'I think we'll get along just fine. There's nothing worse than dissension in the kitchen,' she laughed, and a shrewd look at Jade followed. 'Then that means you're to be Sarah's new companion,' she smiled kindly again, 'and from the look of that red hair of yours, you won't be letting her browbeat you, I shouldn't wonder.'

'Oh, Jade's very even-tempered,' interposed Helen with a chuckle, '. . . for a redhead.' Which made all three of them laugh.

Jenny now indicated a swinging door that was still moving slightly at the end of the passage.

'Perhaps you'd like to come and have some morning tea with me,' she offered, and to Helen, 'See some of your working area, so to speak. I think you'll like it.'

That was an understatement if ever there was one, decided the girls when they followed her into the kitchen

46

seconds later. It was not only one of the largest the
ever seen, but also the best equipped. From what they
see there could hardly have been an appliance on the
market that hadn't been included. There was plenty of
bench space, an abundance of cupboards, and the whole had
been decorated in colonial style. Even the oval polished
table and matching wooden chairs with their colourful cush-
ioned seats that they could see beyond the waist-high room
divider carried the same theme.

'Take a seat,' suggested Jenny pleasantly, 'the coffee's
just about ready,' and in no time at all she had thrown a
small lace cloth over the table and brought out some gold
and brown ironstone cups and saucers, together with a plate
piled high with freshly made lamingtons—delicious confections of sponge cake dipped in chocolate and then rolled in
grated coconut. 'You two don't look as if you have to worry
about your figures, and I gave up on mine years ago,' she
passed the comment ruefully.

After two lamingtons and two cups of coffee each, the
three of them moved back contentedly, Jenny saying, 'If
you want to smoke, go ahead. There's an ashtray on the
divider there. I don't myself, but my Jack does—contin-
ually I might add.'

It was Jade who reached across and picked up the ashtray, but before she could place it on the table the door to
the hallway swung open and Tory McGrath walked into the
room with an easy sinuous stride. He came over to the table
and smiled down at Jenny, making Jade's heart inexplicably begin thumping at her ribs while she studied him
afresh. Up until now she had only been the recipient of a
cool contemptuous arrogance from him, but at the moment
she was seeing him in a completely different mood, and the
change was overwhelming.

'I just came to tell you that I won't be in for lunch,
Jenny. I've got to see Ted Mason, so I'll grab a bite to eat
while I'm there.' His eyes gleamed discerningly at the

lamingtons left on the plate. 'Hmm, they look good,' he remarked to no one in particular, and swiftly two had disappeared into his hand and he was heading back to the door.

'Tory, will there be any extras for dinner tonight?' Jenny called after him.

With one hand resting on the door he turned back, inclining his head towards Jade and Helen. 'Not unless the girls are staying,' he said.

Jade was on her feet in an instant, her colour rising, furious with herself for having given him the opportunity to imply that they were still there in the hopes of a free meal.

He must have guessed what she had been thinking, for he promptly ordered in dry tones, 'Sit down, Jade! That wasn't a hint for you to leave. You're both welcome to stay for dinner if you wish,' and it was his casual use of her first name, as if he had been using it for years, as much as the words he actually uttered, that had Jade resuming her seat in nervous confusion. When she looked up again he was gone.

'You didn't really think that Tory wanted you to leave, did you, dear?' Jenny asked worriedly. 'I can assure you he meant what he said—you are welcome to stay if you wish—it's no trouble. We're used to visitors here.'

'No, really, we must be on our way, thanks very much, Jenny.' It was Helen who rose to her feet this time. 'We've all our packing to do again this afternoon, and we'd already decided on an early night because of the long day we had yesterday.'

'As long as you don't think anyone's rushing you off.'

'No, truly, Jenny, we must go,' Jade spoke up, confirming Helen's words. 'But thanks for the coffee and lamingtons—they were lovely.'

'Tory seemed to think so too,' agreed Jenny with a pleased look.

Their goodbyes said, the girls were speedily on their way

back to town, neither of them actually saying much but rather more deep in their own thoughts. It wasn't until the middle of the afternoon, when they had almost finished their re-packing, that Helen broached the subject that had been on her mind ever since their interviews had been concluded that morning.

'Jade?' she questioned lightly, curling up in a cross-legged position on her bed.

'Umm?'

'You're not really happy about starting work out there tomorrow, are you?'

'Whatever gave you that idea?' Jade kept on with her packing. 'How else could I check up on the Pascoes' gory past?'

'Be serious, Jade. I know there's something wrong. I've never seen you like this before.'

Hardly surprising after the names I was called this morning, mused Jade ruefully. Aloud all she said was, 'You're imagining things, Helen. I'm wildly ecstatic about the thought of working there.'

'No, I'm not imagining things,' Helen declared emphatically. 'As you said to me last night—I've known you too long not to know the signs. There's something bothering you and I mean to find out what it is. If you want to call the whole thing off, then say so! I know I'm a bit gone on Mike at the moment,' she smiled wryly, 'but not so far that I couldn't back out. If that's what's holding you here—don't let it! We're *both* supposed to be having a good holiday.'

Jade flashed her friend an appreciative smile, left her clothes draped over the lid of her suitcase and searched on the top of the dressing table for her cigarettes. Lighting one, she was annoyed to find her fingers shaking slightly. She threw herself flat on to her stomach on the bed.

'Well?' demanded Helen impatiently.

'It's all so stupid really,' murmured Jade reflectively, rolling on to her back and blowing smoke at the ceiling. 'If

49

it was just Sarah I had to contend with maybe it wouldn't be so bad, but that grandson of hers informed me, in no uncertain terms either, that he considers I have a materialistic personality and that I'm a gold-digging hussy—and those are his words, verbatim.'

'Tory said that!' Helen evidently couldn't believe her ears, but at Jade's interrogating lift of one winged eyebrow at the use of their boss's Christian name, murmured defensively. 'He told me to call him that.' Her voice strengthened again almost immediately. 'But why? What reason had he for making such a statement?'

'Because he happened to overhear that comment I made last night in the lounge about looking for "a husband who could afford to keep me", etcetera, etcetera.'

'But didn't you tell him it was only a joke? That it didn't mean anything?'

'Are you kidding? *You* try telling him!' Jade shrugged her shoulders resignedly. 'That was when I was told I was trying to excuse my materialistic personality! Mr McGrath doesn't consider such remarks to be jokes and has arbitrarily decided that I am an undesirable female—probably with loose morals just to complete the picture—and that I'm on the lookout for a wealthy husband into whom I can sink my mercenary claws!'

'You can't be serious!' Helen was aghast.

Another stream of smoke found its way to the ceiling. 'I agree you'd think I wasn't—but I am.' Jade laughed mirthlessly. 'He probably thought it was himself I was after. Now that is a joke!'

'Well, it's obvious we can't work there if that's what he thinks of you.' Helen hopped off her bed and made for the door. 'I'll go downstairs now and phone to say we've changed our minds.'

'How can we after the contracts we signed?'

That had the effect of halting Helen abruptly.

'What contracts?' she queried suspiciously.

Now Jade propped herself up to look closely at her friend. 'Didn't you sign one?' and after Helen's negative shake of her head she lay back down again. 'I wonder why he made me sign one then?'

Again came the inquiry, 'What contract?' but less patiently this time.

'The one guaranteeing to work there for three months. I wouldn't have put my signature to it except that I automatically assumed you'd done the same.'

Helen came back and sat down heavily on the end of the bed. 'Then we're stuck!' she said.

Decisively Jade swung her legs over the side of the bed and stubbed out her cigarette in an ashtray.

'Maybe in that way we are,' she agreed. 'But I'm damned if I'll let Tory McGrath have it all his own way!'

'Why, what are you going to do?'

'I haven't quite made up my mind yet, but one thing you can be sure of, I'll give him a good run for his money. Mr McGrath might, even yet, find me digging for gold among his wealthy guests.'

'Jade! You wouldn't?' protested Helen, delightfully shocked.

'Oh, yes, I would,' laughed Jade, 'if I thought it would annoy the insufferable Tory McGrath. Besides, Dad would be terribly disappointed if I came this far and didn't investigate the Pascoe beginnings.'

'And yet he didn't seem to have it in for you when he came into the kitchen and we were with Jenny,' Helen now mused thoughtfully.

'No doubt putting on a charming act for your and Jenny's benefit. It wouldn't do for all the staff to know his personal opinion of me.'

Helen wandered disconsolately back to her packing. 'I wish it hadn't happened this way, though,' she murmured.

Jade only grinned and hunched her shoulders offhandedly.

'Who knows? It could perhaps be fun yet. You know how the saying goes, "If you've got the name..."'

'Jade! Don't...!' her friend broke in worriedly. 'That would only make things worse!'

Another shrug and a broad grin followed. 'How much worse can they get?' was the flippant reasoning.

CHAPTER FOUR

IT was a little after eight o'clock on Monday morning by the time Jade and Helen had cleared their room of all their belongings, stowed them neatly in the van, paid their hotel bill and said farewell to Mac and Diana.

A Mac who accompanied them to where their vehicle was parked in the front of the building, saying in his own friendly manner, 'Don't forget, if there's anything I can ever do for you, you only have to ask. Good luck to both of you—I think you'll enjoy working at Marandoo. Tory's a fair boss and I've never heard complaints from any of his staff yet.'

Jade opened her mouth, but Helen interrupted quickly before she had a chance to speak.

'Thanks very much, Mac. I'm sure we'll like it,' and giving Jade no opportunity to say anything other than a rushed, 'Cheerio, Mac,' she hastily swung the van away from the hotel and roared down the street leaving spurts of dust to trail behind them. Jade glanced at her companion quizzically and burst into laughter.

'What did you think I was going to say?' she asked sunnily.

Helen slowed their speed down and gave a rueful grin in response.

'I wasn't too sure, but I wasn't intending to hang around and find out either! I thought discretion dictated that we make an immediate departure. I know what you're like when you do lose that redheaded temper of yours.'

'I haven't done that for ages,' returned Jade complacently, sweeping ruffled curls from her forehead.

'N-o,' admitted Helen slowly, 'but I thought it might be about due.'

Now Jade's mouth took on a wry turn. 'Shame on you, Helen Nye, for even suggesting such a thing,' she teased. 'I was perfectly composed and in control of my sometimes volatile emotions. Believe me, if I do happen to lose it, I know exactly where the full force will be directed ... straight at one very overbearing, over-confident, and over-wealthy male!'

'Poor Tory!'

'Poor Tory be damned! Look at all the things he accused me of!'

'And look at all the things you've just accused him of!'

Jade conceded the point with another laugh. 'I'm as bad as he is, aren't I?' Followed incorrigibly by, 'But then he's proved he's all of those things I said, whereas I haven't.'

'But I suppose to someone who does have a lot of money, that remark you made could go against the grain,' Helen tried hard to be strictly unprejudiced and view the matter from both sides. 'It would be horrible to discover that someone had married you just because they wanted your money.'

'Well, that's hardly a problem that's ever likely to worry us, and from the little that I've had to do with him I should imagine that would be the *only* reason why anyone would want to marry Tory McGrath. I'm not surprised he's still single.'

Now it was Helen's turn to laugh. 'Jade, I've never heard you so biased! You couldn't possibly believe that! Even you would have to agree that Tory's one of the most attractive males we've seen in a long time. He wouldn't be hard up for girl-friends even if he didn't have a penny to his name,' she finished categorically.

A grudging, 'Maybe,' was all she received for an answer from a Jade who reluctantly recalled her first impression obtained in the hotel. But looks could be so deceptive, she kept telling herself, and the recollection of his attitude towards her during the interview helped to bolster her determination not to be swayed by sheer physical appeal.

Shortly afterwards they had pulled up close to the back entrance of the homestead, where Jenny came happily out to greet them, a short fair-haired man dressed in work clothes following close behind her.

'This is Jack, my husband,' she explained and, the rest of the introductions completed, 'He'll carry your cases upstairs for you. Is there anything else you want out of the van?'

Again the girls pulled out a couple of smaller bags and followed Jenny into the house and up the wide curving staircase, with Jack bringing up the rear and their larger pieces of luggage. At the top of the stairs Jenny led them down the left-hand gallery, pointing out, 'That's Sarah's suite,' on the way. Next they stopped and Jenny showed them into what was to be Jade's room.

It was beautifully furnished in rich-toned wood with the bed an imitation colonial four-poster, although Jade suspected the imitation cost far more than an original would have done, covered by a pale green, lemon and white printed voile bedspread with a quilted top and a deeply gathered valance. The fitted wardrobe with its louvre doors reached almost the entire length of one wall, while the matching dressing table supported an enormous swinging mirror, and in one corner there stood a small writing table partnered by a comfortable-looking chair. Another louvred door set in one wall concealed her own bathroom, while the floors were of gleaming wood, covered here and there by pale green fluffy mats. At least she could find no fault with her accommodation, Jade reflected with a pleasurable acceptance.

Jack deposited her luggage in the room and then Jenny once again showed the way to the end of the hall where she opened the door to another room. This was wallpapered in a Regency design of pale pink and blue flowers between vertical stripes of a palest rose, with a deep orchid-pink carpet which perfectly toned with the soft throwover style bedspread of the same colouring. Jade noticed that Helen too had her own bathroom and that the views from both their windows were the same in that they looked over the waving grass to the heat-shrouded hills in the distance.

'I expect you'd like to unpack and settle in a bit first,' Jenny was saying, 'so when you've finished you can come down to me in the kitchen and we'll take it from there. If you ever want me at any time and I'm not downstairs, that's Jack's and my suite of rooms across the hallway,' and she indicated a door almost opposite Helen's own.

Directly Jenny and her husband had left the girls exchanged pleased grins and Jade departed to do her own unpacking. This time, knowing that her stay was to be of some duration, she removed everything from her cases and after smoothing out as many creases as she could, hung her clothes carefully in the long wardrobe, mentally making a note to ask Jenny if she might use the iron. She had soon finished, and turned to survey her reflection in the giant mirror, scrutinising her slim figure in buttercup yellow flared pants with a white and yellow polka-dotted top and white wedge-heeled sandals. Leaning forward slightly, she ran a comb through her deeply waving hair and added an extra touch of bronze lipstick to her mouth. On standing back she shrugged faintly—that would have to do—then she turned and left the room.

In the kitchen Jade found Helen there before her, already helping Jenny with mid-morning coffee. A tray was sitting on one of the benches with two cups and saucers, a plate of sliced dark fruit cake as well as one of feathery light sponge fingers, a sugar bowl and a jug of thick rich cream already on it. Jenny finished pouring the liquid into a tall slim coffee pot and placed it beside the cups.

'Sarah said you'd be having your morning coffee with

her, so I thought you might like to take it along,' said Jenny. 'She's in the library—where you saw her yesterday.'

Jade nodded compliance and with a 'Here we go' look directed at Helen pushed out through the swing door and down the hall to the library. She knocked quietly, but firmly, and waited until she'd heard Sarah's imperative, 'Enter,' before turning the handle.

'Ah, there you are,' Sarah greeted her brusquely as Jade moved into the room and placed the tray on the table between the armchair and the sofa. 'Thought I might have scared you off yesterday and you wouldn't put in an appearance.'

Deciding on the spur of the moment that she wasn't going to be browbeaten by two members of the McGrath family, Jade retorted swiftly with a dry smile,

'And were you hoping you *had* frightened me off?'

'Of course not!' came the slightly testy reply, and an even testier, 'Sit down, girl, sit down! I'm not royalty—you don't have to stand in my presence.' And when Jade had taken a seat on the sofa, 'You can pour, and while you're doing it you can tell me why you thought I might want to scare you away.'

Having the discussion thrown back at her so abruptly caught Jade unawares, but by the time she'd ascertained that Sarah liked her coffee black and sweet, had poured both cups and added cream to her own, she had her thoughts well marshalled.

'I wasn't actually sure that you did when I was speaking to you. It was rather that I had the impression you were trying to startle me into saying something damaging.' She took a mouthful of coffee and lifted her shoulders passively. 'It wasn't until later that I discovered the reason why.'

'And that was?'

It was now or never and Jade faced her questioner resolutely.

'Because your grandson believes I came out here with the

sole purpose of finding myself a rich husband.' There, it was out! Let her make of it what she liked!

'*Was* that your idea?' barked Sarah.

Jade found herself flushing under the piercing blue-eyed gaze and she hastened to deny the implication.

'No, it wasn't! I had nothing of the sort in mind—I don't even *want* to get married.'

'What? Not ever?'

A faint smile tugged at the corners of Jade's mouth at this interpretation.

'Well, not for a long time yet, anyway,' she asserted. 'I would, at least, like to finish this trip we started on first.'

'No man waiting for you ... where was it your friend Helen said ... in Melbourne?' Sarah inquired in softer tones.

At the thought of Lionel Wilson—her last casual boy-friend—a frown crossed Jade's forehead. He would be waiting for her, although she'd told him not to, but she didn't think that was what Sarah meant.

'No, not really,' she told her at last.

'Hah!' Sarah pounced on her indecision. 'Wishy-washy type who lets you get away with murder, I suppose ... and that's no good for *you*! What you need, my girl, is a man who can control you, and, unless I miss my guess, you'd be a handful for any man to manage—especially if he was in love with you!' she went on with the audacious tongue of the elderly.

None too sure just how they had got on to the subject of her love-life, but relieved at the change in Sarah's manner, Jade found herself genuinely amused at that lady's thoughts on the matter. However, she also thought a change might be prudent before Sarah had a further opportunity to expound her theories.

'I love your home—it's very beautiful,' she compli-mented earnestly.

Sarah snorted disgruntledly before a faint acknowledging

twinkle came to light in the depths of those very blue eyes.

'Quite adept at changing course, aren't you? And the house isn't mine—it belongs to Tory.'

'But you've always lived here?'

'Ever since I married Tory's grandfather.' Her eyes drifted reminiscently to the windows and the far distant horizon. 'I have another house on the coast which we had built many years ago, but with all the holidaymakers and tourists invading the area during the summer months it's not the same any more—the peace and quiet enjoyment have gone. That's why I like it here ... it's restful.'

Jade could sympathise with the older woman. After the rush and hectic scramble of life in the city, Marandoo seemed a haven of tranquillity, and she said as much to Sarah.

'And you think you'll be able to stand the solitude for three months? Most girls your age would be only too anxious to return to the city after a couple of weeks out here.'

'I wouldn't exactly describe it as solitude,' laughed Jade. 'There are too many people around on the property, and it's not so very far to town.'

'But it's the same faces—week in, week out. Even when you go to town there's very little variety,' Sarah took pains to point out grimly. 'That's what usually sends them all packing in the end—lack of choice. Some can't stand it— affects them like claustrophobia—they feel they have to leave or they're going to suffocate.'

'I can't see it affecting me that way,' Jade answered thoughtfully. Besides, she'd stick it out just to spite that grandson of Sarah's, even if it killed her! 'Of course we've only been here since Saturday,' she went on, 'so it hasn't really been a test, but I think I'd love the life. No neighbours to peep at you from behind pulled curtains every time your front door opens or closes—I couldn't imagine anything better.'

'You don't like your neighbours?'

'The Nyes, Helen's people, live on one side of us and they're really nice, but,' here Jade grimaced expressively, 'on the other side live the Mulhollands, and she's the greatest busybody that ever drew breath. Every time you take a step out of doors she's either watching from her windows or she's hanging over the fence wanting to know where you're going, who with, and what the rest of the family are doing. She's a real menace!'

Sarah nodded knowingly. 'I'm aware of the type, but somehow I don't think you'll suffer the same sort of interference out here.' A slight smile appeared. 'We can't even see our neighbours' homesteads, let alone know whether they're inside or outside of them.'

Before either of them could say anything further the door opened and a tall dark-haired girl of about twenty-six years of age breezed into the room, a cup and saucer balanced shakily in one hand. It didn't take much deduction on Jade's part to work out that this must be Tory's sister, Barbara, for the family resemblance was very noticeable. Apart from the same dark hair, which Barbara wore in a neatly styled pageboy, there were the same grey eyes, although she did have a distinct tinge of blue to hers, but the bone structure was the same—only this time more softly defined—and the finely shaped mouth held the same sensual curve as that of her elder brother. She was wearing what was obviously a most expensively tailored slacks suit in a glorious cyclamen colour which suited her to perfection.

Plumping down on the couch next to Jade, Barbara flashed them both a dazzling white smile and pushed her empty cup and saucer on to the table.

'I've come to meet your new companion, Sarah, and to have my coffee with you,' she told her grandmother brightly. 'I hope you haven't drunk it all yet.'

'Help yourself,' invited Sarah, her eyes softening as they

rested affectionately on the attractive picture her grand-daughter made as she and Jade made each other free with their first names and Barbara poured herself a cup of coffee, liberally adding cream and sugar.

Sarah waved aside Jade's offer to refill her cup, asking Barbara instead, 'And what have you been doing with yourself this morning?'

'I went for a ride early with Tory and had to come home on my own,' with a laughing grimace, 'because he found part of the fence down in the Reach paddock which, of course, he just had to attend to there and then. After breakfast,' she smiled evocatively, 'I received a phone call from Nigel,' an aside to Jade of, '... that's my fiancé-to-be, Nigel Sayers ... saying he can't possibly make it up here for at least another fortnight yet. I was thinking of asking Tory to fly me to Brisbane on Wednesday seeing that Nigel can't get away, and there are still a few things I want to arrange with the caterers.' She tilted her head to one side inquiringly, gauging what sort of reaction she would obtain from Sarah to this idea.

'Oh, yes, of course, we mustn't forget the caterers, must we?' smiled her grandmother in lively understanding. 'Go, if you want to—you'll only be wandering around with a long sad face if you don't—but you must call and see your Aunt Ellen while you're there or she'll never forgive you, especially now that she can't make it to your party,' instructed Sarah, while Jade sat back amazed at the ease with which they spoke of flying to Brisbane as if it were a common occurrence, which, of course, she chided herself wryly, it probably was for the McGraths and other wealthy families like them. This was seeing how the other half lived—and with a vengeance.

'And while I'm in Brisbane I can post the invitations,' Barbara went on happily, already envisaging her pleasurable reunion with Nigel.

'What? Haven't you sent them yet?' Sarah questioned

with a darkening frown. 'Really, Barbara, they should have gone last week at the latest! I've never known anyone who procrastinates quite so much as you do.'

'Well, it wasn't all my fault,' Barbara felt bound to protest with a shamefaced grin. 'I had arranged for Gwen to type the envelopes out for me last Wednesday but,' she moved her hands resignedly, 'you know how ill she was feeling last week and I couldn't ask her then to do them for me.'

'Did it ever occur to you that you might write them out by hand?'

'Well, yes, it had occurred to me,' conceded her rueful, but unabashed, granddaughter. 'But after having filled out all those invitations, the mere thought of writing out the envelopes as well gave me the cold shudders.' Her white smile darted at Jade and Sarah in turn before she cajoled, 'I was wondering if you could lend me Jade for the afternoon so that they could be finished today.' She faced the girl next to her. 'If you don't mind?'

Jade certainly didn't mind and said so. After all, that was what she had been employed for. She was there to work, not to be treated as a guest.

'I suppose so,' Sarah yielded indulgently to the transference of her companion, then with more determination, 'But you make sure you finish all of them. I don't want any more excuses, Barbara—they must be posted in Brisbane on Wednesday.'

'As good as done,' Barbara twinkled irrepressibly. 'I'll take all the necessary down to the office after lunch and I'll meet you there, Jade. That okay?'

'Sure,' Jade confirmed hollowly, trying hard to keep her forced smile from slipping.

Did it have to be the office? Couldn't it have been somewhere else? She knew that in her secretarial capacity she would have to use it sometime, but she had thought to have at least her first day on the property free from Tory's critical proximity. She sighed and surreptitiously crossed her fingers. Perhaps, with luck, he would be out working all afternoon.

Another knock sounded on the library door, and a moment later a flushed and bright-eyed Helen walked into the room.

'I've come to collect the tray, Mrs McGrath ... if you've finished.'

'Oh, you'd better call her Sarah,' laughed Barbara, giving her grandmother a broad grin, 'everyone does. Says she can't see the point in having a Christian name if no one ever uses it.'

Helen glanced undecidedly from Barbara to Sarah and back again, whereupon the elder McGrath smiled graciously, saying, 'Yes, call me Sarah, child. As my irreclaimable granddaughter has just informed you, everyone else does.' Her gaze transferred to the girl still seated on the couch. 'You too, Jade. We stand on no ceremony here.'

Shortly after Helen's departure Barbara rose to her feet and headed for the door also.

'I think I'll go upstairs and sort through my wardrobe— see what I ought to take with me to Brisbane,' she told them. 'I'll see you both at lunch,' and with a brief smile she was gone.

Sarah leant across and picked up a thick book which had been resting on the coffee table.

'I'm glad you like reading,' she smiled at Jade, making the younger girl realise just how attractive Sarah must have been in her heyday, 'because my eyes aren't what they used to be and I don't like wearing my glasses, so I thought you could read aloud to me. I think you might like this book too—it's quite humorous.'

Taking the volume from Sarah's outstretched hand, Jade turned to the page where a fringed leather bookmark had been inserted and began to read. It wasn't long before both she and Sarah were chuckling quietly as the story unfolded and the comical characters involved themselves in one hilarious situation after another, and by the time lunch was ready Jade was as amusedly engrossed in the tale as Sarah.

Only the three women were seated at the oval table for lunch, making Jade wonder whether her finger-crossing had succeeded. She certainly hoped so! Helen, she supposed, would be having her meals with Jenny and Jack in the kitchen. Jade too would have preferred to take her meals where she could escape from the eagle eye of the master of the house, but she hadn't been given the choice. She was only hopeful that his immediate absence from the table was not an unusual event.

However, for all the lack of diners, there was no lack of conversation, and with Barbara regaling Jade with various titbits of gossip and supposed scandal that buzzed around the station and outlying districts, with Sarah's own sharp wit tossed in periodically, the meal passed quickly and pleasantly.

Afterwards Sarah told Jade that she normally had a rest in the afternoons—sometimes of a short duration, sometimes long—and having seen that lady comfortably settled on her bed and the blinds drawn, Jade hurried back downstairs and into the office. With a little bit more luck she might be able to finish her work before Tory returned.

With a flourish she removed the cover from the electric typewriter and folded it neatly while swivelling to and fro on the padded typist's chair behind the second desk in the room. This was placed some distance from, but sideways to, the leather-covered desk that Tory had used for her interview and, should the need ever arise, Jade noted that she could covertly watch the other desk without actually appearing to be so doing. Of course, she reminded herself with a grimace, any person seated at the other desk could do exactly the same in return.

By the time she had checked through the desk drawers to enlighten herself as to what stationery and equipment they held, Barbara had walked into the room holding aloft a large square cardboard box.

'I think everything's here,' she smiled at Jade, and placed the box on the edge of the desk. Plunging in her hand, she brought forth a thick wad of foolscap pages covered in handwritten names and addresses and handed it to Jade. 'That's for the envelopes,' she explained. 'But don't worry about finding the right invitations for the right envelopes— I can do all that tomorrow. I'm only too pleased at not having to write them out by hand. Do you think you'll be able to finish them all in one afternoon?'

Jade rifled through the pages quickly and nodded her head. 'I should think so,' she said. 'How many are there?'

Barbara hunched her shoulders, her eyebrows rising as she smiled.

'I don't really know. We had two hundred printed but, of course, most of those are doubles, and there are still some in the box that I haven't used. Actually I have no idea what the number came to in the end.'

'Okay,' Jade laughed. 'I'll see how I go and I can total them up once I've finished.'

'Thanks a lot, Jade. It really will be a load off my mind once they're in the post. Sarah's right in what she said about me this morning—I do tend to put things off and there's always a rush at the last minute.' She started to smile. 'I hate to think what I'll be like on my wedding day!'

Left on her own Jade rolled a sheet of paper into the typewriter and did a few practice runs to get the feel of the unfamiliar machine before she began on the expensive parchment envelopes that were to be distributed, judging by her earlier perfunctory glance, to just about every State and Territory of the Commonwealth.

An hour and a half later Jade had a steadily increasing pile of finished work beside her, but there was still a long way to go and she began to think that she might not, after all, complete the list that afternoon. Although she was used to an electric typewriter, this wasn't a model she had used before, and also she occasionally had to stop and puzzle over Barbara's handwriting—quite apart from the fact that as the sun made its slow descent in the afternoon sky it was burning its way into that particular part of the building. The atmosphere in the office was becoming distinctly torrid and she had opened the windows wider in an endeavour to find some small relief from the scorching rays.

Suddenly the door of the office was thrust open and Tory, dressed in creased and dusty wide-belted jeans and pale blue shirt, swung into the room with a long lithe stride. On seeing Jade seated behind the secondary desk he stopped and ran a hand roughly through dark tousled hair.

'My God!' he expostulated. 'What are you trying to do? Turn the place into a sauna?'

Jade lifted startled eyes from the envelope she had been about to type and looked at him in some consternation. What was she supposed to have done now? As far as she was aware the sun had been doing that quite adequately without any help from her.

Moving behind his desk, Tory slammed both windows closed before stepping across to an attractive painting on the wall where he flipped back a side panel to turn a switch before setting the panel back in place. With lean fingers resting lightly on slim sensual hips, he demanded, 'Why didn't you turn the air-conditioning on?'

Now he tells me, fumed Jade. After having struggled on all this time in the sweltering heat! She stared at him rebelliously.

'Had I known it was there, I _would_ have done so, Mr McGrath!' she snapped sarcastically.

A scathing look came her way as he pointed to the now obvious air vents above the painting.

'In that case, what did you think they were for? And the switches in the panel?'

The draughts of cooling air that were beginning to enter the room were in no way helping to reduce Jade's heightened temperature and she gave him back a look as scornful as his own.

'As much as this might surprise you, *Mr McGrath*, I came in here to do some work for Barbara ... not to make an inspection of the wall paintings and the general fittings!' She waved a hand towards the wall. 'It didn't occur to me to look over there to see if the room was air-conditioned. Besides,' she gibed sweetly, 'when a place is air-conditioned the windows aren't usually open.'

'That's in offices and other large buildings. I happen to prefer to have a choice. In the mornings when it's cool I like to have the windows open.'

With a scornful smile Jade turned back to her typing, muttering, 'How nice for you!' under her breath.

'*Jade!*'

The word came across deeply and smoothly, but there was a steely warning in it all the same that sent icy shivers down Jade's spine, although she steadfastly refused to look at him and concentrated her gaze on the envelope in the typewriter.

'Don't try pushing me too hard, or you might find the outcome too much for you to handle!'

Now she did look at him—stormily! Don't push *him* too far! What about him pushing *her*! It was on the tip of her tongue to continue her opposition when she noticed the expectant half-smile playing about his mouth and the challenging look in the smoky grey eyes that had her heart rate increasing alarmingly while he leant back, aggravatingly confident, with his hands clasped at the back of his head.

Strangely her antagonism faded away and she murmured. 'Yes, Mr McGrath,' in a suitably repressed tone.

Tory now moved forward in his chair to rest his forearms along the desk top.

'And, Jade ..., he waited until she looked up and then he

laughed, a deep attractive sound, 'you'd better make it Tory. I wouldn't like to make it too obvious that we're indulging in a private feud. It might raise questions that both of us would prefer to remain unanswered.'

'If you say so, Mr McGrath,' Jade replied through gritted teeth.

Oh, no, of course he wouldn't want it generally known that he had it in for her—that might spoil his carefully-built image of courteous charm that he reserved for the other members of his female staff.

'Jade!'

Her eyes flickered and fell beneath the amused tolerance in his own, hating his easy self-assurance, while she felt a mass of quivering hesitations and unco-ordinated thoughts. It was evident he had no intention of allowing her to defy his authority, but Jade's tumultuous emotions weren't ready to accept his male dominance either—no matter how fascinatingly packaged!

'Jade!'

When it came the second time his voice held more command but the same lazy smile clung to his curving mouth, and although she tried to outstare him, in the end it was her eyes that fell once more and she agreed finally, 'Yes, Tory,' in husky defeat.

'Right ... now let's see ...' He began sorting through a great pile of papers on his desk, interrupting Jade's recommenced typing with, 'Have you much to do for Barbara?'

'Only the envelopes for her party invitations,' she answered, as coolly formal as possible.

'That's good. I'll get you to take some notes and maybe I can finally get some of this work moving.'

Tory evidently wasn't aware of the number of invitations, or else he surmised that she was further through them than she actually was. For a moment or two she contemplated telling him how much of his sister's work she still had to finish, but on second thoughts decided not to.

After all, to be strictly fair, he was paying her wages, not Barbara, and as she had always been carefully taught, right from her days in college, that company correspondence always took precedence over private letters, she merely retrieved a notebook from a drawer of her desk, picked up a pencil, and went to sit in the same chair she had occupied during that—she hoped—never-to-be-repeated interview.

For the next hour Tory kept up a steady stream of dictation that filled page after page of Jade's notebook with neat hieroglyphics and disposed of a large proportion of his accumulated mail. When he finally leant back in his chair, clearly well pleased with the amount he had concluded, Jade almost dreaded the answer to any secretary's well-worn query, 'Did you want these this afternoon?'

'If possible, please, Jade.' He rose to his feet and moved around to her side of the desk, looking down at her lowered head. 'I've got to go out again now, so just leave them on my desk when you've finished and I'll sign them either later today or early tomorrow morning—then young Eric can take them w.th him when he goes into town.'

Jade nodded silently and saw his long muscular legs move out of her line of vision as he headed towards the door while she heaved a deep sigh of dismay. How on earth was she going to get both lots done? Oh, well, it was her own fault for not having mentioned the amount she still had left to do for Barbara, but if she had no more interruptions she just might manage to get the greater percentage done for both of them.

The sun was beginning to set into a ball of molten fire and the shadows in the office had darkened to violet before Jade at last completed Tory's letters and laid the tidy pile in the middle of his desk. Switching on the overhead light, she picked up a cigarette from her drawer, lit it, and went to stand beside the windows, looking out into the increasing darkness while she stretched her legs and back. She wasn't used, nowadays, to sitting in one position for so long. In a very short time the sun had disappeared altogether and left the navy-blue clouds tinged with red and gold against a dimming azure sky. Stubbing out her cigarette, she returned to her desk and pulled Barbara's box of invitations towards her once more.

She had only added another ten to her growing collection when the door was vigorously opened and Tory stood in the entrance with one hand still resting on the handle. A Tory who clearly had showered and changed since she had seen him last, for his hair had a damp curling look to it and he was now wearing a pair of slim-fitting dark brown pants with an oatmeal-coloured short-sleeved silk knit shirt. But it was also a Tory who was controlling his temper with some difficulty.

'What the hell are you playing at, Jade?' he bit out angrily.

Jade's eyes widened warily. What now? Was she always to be confronted by enigmatic interrogations the moment they came into contact? He was impatiently waiting for an answer and, in defence, she resorted to sarcasm.

'I had thought I was playing the role of conscientious secretary,' she told him with heavy mockery. 'However, from the look on your face I gather I'm about to be told that I've been labouring under a misapprehension.' She glared at him mutinously, her eyes sparkling furiously. 'What am I *supposed* to have done *now*?' she inquired.

Tory swung the door closed forcefully and came to stand before her desk, leaning his strong hands flat on the top, bending towards her and cautioning her with a slight shake of his head.

'Don't push your luck, Jade! I'm in no mood for it! I've had both Sarah and Barbara on my back for the past half-hour accusing me of being a slave-driver by giving you so much work that you couldn't find time to have your afternoon tea and you don't appear to be coming to dinner ... especially when you had Barbara's invitations to do as

70

well.' His glance was cold. 'Would you mind telling me why you didn't see fit to inform me of that fact?'

The idea of both Sarah and Barbara defending her to Tory brought a tiny smile to Jade's lips and she answered insouciantly, 'You didn't ask me.'

Neither the smile nor the reply was appreciated, for Tory leant a little closer until Jade could see quite plainly the midnight pupil in his clear grey eyes with their long black lashes, and the fine pencil drawn lines radiating from the corners, caused by long hours spent in brilliant sunlight.

She could see quite plainly too the wrathful heat contained within those eyes as he snapped, 'I shouldn't have to! You've got a tongue in your head! One which you haven't been averse to using, either, up until now!'

His nearness was having a strange effect upon Jade's senses; she could feel her pulse increasing its tempo and her breath was coming in short shallow gulps. Annoyed that she had allowed him to affect her to such an extent, she edged backwards on her chair, lifted her head high and gave him back look for look.

'And I'm not afraid of using it again if I have to,' she declared heatedly. 'Just for your information, I stupidly thought that as you were paying my wages you had prior claim on my services. You see, Tory McGrath, I do happen to have some principles, strange though it may seem to you!' Jade felt perilously close to tears and dragged her gaze away to stare down at her desk, blinking hard to keep them at bay, and murmuring huskily, 'But evidently that was wrong too!'

A short laugh escaped Tory. 'Principles! You?' he scoffed sardonically. 'If you think you can pull the wool over my eyes by putting on the "loyal employee" act, you're very much mistaken, Jade. I've met too many girls who've come out west with the intention of hooking an unsuspecting male to ever be taken in by one.'

Jade's hand clenched into a fist as his derogatory words

71

washed over her. She would have liked to take a swing at him, but as it was she was too busy trying to keep back the salty tears threatening to burst forth humiliatingly at any moment. She would not allow him the chance to congratulate himself on having made her cry!

Tory's eyes narrowed thoughtfully as he watched the downcast head before him, curving lashes shading rose-tinted creamy-skinned cheeks, pearly white teeth biting at an enticingly soft lower lip. He straightened and ran a hand around the back of his neck irritatedly.

'I did say you need only finish those letters today if it was possible,' he sighed, reverting to his reason for being there.

Jade lifted glittering eyes that shimmered with the translucent glow of her namesake and reproached him wryly.

'Is that supposed to be an apology?'

'For what?'

'Your unwarranted behaviour.'

Obviously it wasn't.

'Any behaviour you receive from me is only what you bring on yourself and what you deserve. Anyone with an outlook like yours is entitled to no better! As far as I can see, you're Jade by name and a jade by nature!' he told her contemptuously.

The fiercely muttered, 'I'll make you sorry for that, Tory McGrath,' was out before Jade realised with a hasty swallow that she'd actually said it aloud, and then she gasped, as without giving her an inkling of his intentions Tory had leant across the desk to grab hold of one of her wrists and hauled her out of her chair and around the furniture until she was brought to a sudden halt beside him. His free hand settled in her hair, dragging her head back painfully.

'You little...' he bit off an expletive as two tears overflowed and rolled slowly and searingly down Jade's cheeks. 'Will you stop riding me?' A rueful smile tilted his beguiling mouth. 'It's an unfair fight, you know, and my hand's been itching to tan that pretty hide of yours ever since I first set eyes on you. One of these days you'll force me into doing just that.'

'Don't you ever dare!' Jade lashed back fierily, her tears drying on her crimsoning cheeks at the thought of his presuming to inflict such a belittling punishment. 'Or I'll never speak to you again!' came the dormant threat from childhood before she could stop it.

He started laughing and cupped her face between two warm hands. 'Is that a promise?' he drawled lazily.

Jade could only stare at him wordlessly. The look in his eyes and the feel of his hands against her skin were doing peculiar things to her equilibrium, while her stomach seemed to have gone on an acrobatic spree as, for one wild moment, she thought he was going to lower that dark head and kiss her. How ridiculous could she get? She must be feeling light-headed from the want of food, she decided irritably, pulling away from the unbalancing caress of Tory's fingers. She really would have to be imagining things to think that he would want to kiss *her*, especially when she knew exactly what he thought of her! She shook her head bemusedly, still saying nothing in response to the laughing question in his eyes. For once she was completely speechless.

With a return to his cool indifference Tory again took hold of Jade's wrist, but this time with a lighter grip than before, and began pulling her after him towards the door.

'I'm surprised Sarah and Barbara haven't been along as well to see what's keeping you. You'd better get yourself into the dining room and have your dinner, or my life won't be worth living for the rest of the evening either,' he commented with dry humour.

He strode quickly along the passageway and began talking again, more to himself it seemed than to Jade.

'I knew you were going to be trouble,' he muttered resignedly, then glancing over his shoulder to where she was still trailing him, 'You don't happen to have had ancestors who came from around these parts, do you?' but he had turned away again before she had a chance to reply and didn't see her head nodding affirmatively at his back when he led her into the dining-room.

As she evidently wasn't going to be given the opportunity to wash, change, or even tidy herself, Jade made the best of her appearance by brushing back the unruly curls from her forehead with a slightly unsteady hand and smoothing her yellow and white top tidily down over slim flaring hips before meeting the combined gaze of the two already seated at the table.

No doubt they had been aware of her having to disengage her faintly reddened wrist from a firm grasp, and there was nothing she could do to disguise the unmistakable glimmer of unshed tears that still glistened in her eyes when she took her place at the table, but she forced herself to smile lightly and apologise to Barbara in as calm a voice as she could muster.

'I'm sorry I haven't quite finished your invitations yet, but I'll do them this evening for you. It shouldn't take very long.'

Barbara smiled and was about to speak, but Sarah cut into the conversation before she had a chance to say anything.

'No, you won't,' she ordered shortly, and gave her grandson a baleful glare, which had no effect on him at all, for he merely returned it with a tolerant grin. 'You're my companion first, secretary second. You weren't employed so that you could slave away for every waking hour in that office of Tory's. You can finish Barbara's invitations tomorrow. She should have had them done herself by now anyway,' she finished with a barbed smile at her granddaughter.

Clearly her two grandchildren knew Sarah well, for neither of them seemed at all put out by her looks or her

74

words. In response Barbara pulled a laughing face and gave a wink that encompassed both her brother and Jade, while Tory continued to smile indulgently.

'And just what are you planning to do this evening that necessitates having Jade by your side?' he asked of Sarah.

'Watching television,' she told him with a complacent smile.

It wasn't so very long ago that Sarah would have snorted disgustedly at the idea of anyone watching the television for as many hours as she had over the last twelve months or so, but as her arthritic condition had deteriorated she now took great pleasure from the entertainment it afforded and looked forward to seeing her particular favourites each time they appeared.

One of Tory's eyebrows tilted questioningly. 'And for that you need Jade with you?'

'Maybe ... maybe not,' Sarah replied vaguely, smoothly non-committal. 'But by the look on Jade's face when she entered the dining room I'd say she'd had enough of your company for one day,' wryly, 'and as you are, no doubt, going to spend the rest of the evening in that confounded office as you do almost every other night, I thought it would be best for Jade to be with me.'

At the thought of becoming the subject of a general discussion—as well as dreading what Tory might say—Jade lowered her eyes to the plate in front of her, toying with the food absently while she felt the betraying colour flooding into her face once more that day.

'Perhaps Jade would prefer to do something other than watch T.V.,' Tory's voice suggested drily in the lull.

Jade's eyes immediately flashed upwards, watching Tory warily and hurrying to assure them, 'No. No, there's nothing else I want to do.'

'Not seeing Gary tonight?'

There was a sardonic look to his face that she took exception to, knowing herself to be the subject of interested looks from Sarah and Barbara, and she repeated a stony, 'No! Is there any reason why I should?'

Tory's shoulders rose suggestively and to Jade the implication was plain. As far as he was concerned she was the type that once having caught *any* man's attention would never let go, but this was so far from the actual truth that Jade was a little at a loss as to how best to defend herself, and she was unaware of the hurt bewilderment that showed in her eyes as her glance swept the other members of the room. Luckily Sarah came to her rescue.

'Stop baiting the child, Tory,' she commanded in an exasperated tone. 'She's not experienced enough to be crossing swords with you.'

'Exactly what I keep telling Jade myself, but she seems —er—reluctant to take my advice,' he taunted lazily. 'Perhaps you can convince her of the wisdom of so doing.'

'Don't be so sarcastic, Tory,' Barbara now admonished her brother cheerfully, 'or we'll find Jade wanting to hand in her notice before the week's out.'

'Oh, I don't think so,' he murmured softly, causing his sister and grandmother to stare at him puzzledly, but his glance was locked with Jade's and one corner of his mouth curved knowingly.

Jade refused to respond to that smile. She knew Tory was remembering the contract she had so rashly signed and she could only guess at the enjoyment he must have been finding in the situation where there was no escape for her from his scarcely veiled taunts. She slanted her chin at him disrespectfully, her expression telling him as plainly as words that she didn't consider herself beaten yet—she didn't have her coloured hair for nothing—but it was a little disconcerting to hear him laugh softly at her before Jenny came in to remove their plates.

The rest of the meal proceeded quietly, although Jade took no further part in any conversation, preferring to concentrate on trying to force some food past the lump that had materialised within her throat, but in the end she had eaten very little of the painstakingly prepared meal.

It was, therefore, with some relief that she accompanied Sarah from the dining room, leaving Tory to continue his office work and Barbara to make another phone call to Nigel, and the two of them made themselves comfortable in what Sarah termed 'the family room'. It was the only room in the house completely set aside for the use of the family and not for guests.

A short time later Jenny bustled in, carrying a tray adorned with a polished silver coffee service and a small dish of richly coated dinner mints. After she had left the room and Jade had poured two cups of the deliciously fragrant coffee, Sarah pointed to the mints.

'Have some,' she urged, placing a couple on her own saucer. 'Jenny makes them herself and I can recommend them. Usually I'm not very partial to chocolate, but these are in a different category. After-dinner coffee isn't the same without them.'

Jade still felt as though she couldn't eat a thing, but to please Sarah she tasted one of Jenny's confections and had to admit that they were very more-ish, but her thoughts were far removed from any ideas that could be cooked up in a kitchen. While more of the disturbing daily news unfolded across the wide television screen, Jade's mind roamed along tortuous routes. While she now thought she might come to really like the idea of working for Sarah— she didn't have quite so much the semblance of a fire-eating dragon now as she had yesterday—Jade was deeply concerned over her ability to endure Tory's taunts and gibes for the next three months. At the time of signing the contract thirteen week's hadn't sounded such a long time, but with only one day of that undertaking having elapsed she very much doubted whether she could stand another ninety of the same. She sighed and absently stirred her coffee for the third time. If only Tory had let her explain!

77

It wasn't until Sarah spoke that Jade had any idea that she might have been watching the worried looks chasing each other across her seriously composed face.

'Don't worry too much over what Tory says to you, child,' she interrupted the earnest-faced young man giving weather details on the screen before them. 'Just let me know if he becomes too dominating and I'll give him a piece or two of *my* mind.'

Not doubting that Sarah would be as good as her word, and in no doubts that Tory definitely would not appreciate his grandmother taking up such cudgels in her defence, Jade was aghast at the idea of what trouble *that* would cause.

'Oh, no, Sarah,' she protested quickly, vehemently. 'Please don't do that. I can handle it. It really doesn't matter what Tory thinks of me.' And in the heat of the moment she actually believed what she was saying. 'I wouldn't like to be the cause of any trouble between the two of you.'

'Bless you, child.' Sarah surprisingly leant over and patted Jade consolingly on the hand, but her eyes were twinkling disarmingly. 'I can handle my grandson.' Here she broke into a reminiscent chuckle. 'Of course, I'd have to admit that he knows how to handle me too, but the McGraths were never ones to hold grudges. You can always be sure that if you have an argument with Tory, no matter how fierce, he'll never hold it against you the next day.'

'But it's not exactly an argument we're having,' Jade felt bound to point out. 'It's just that he refuses to believe that I'm not what he thinks I am. And I don't know how to go about convincing him of that.'

'I thought you just said you didn't care what he thought of you,' Sarah reminded her shrewdly.

Jade hunched her shoulders, flushing slightly. 'Well, I guess we all like everyone to think the best of us. It's not very pleasant working for someone who considers you applied for the position under false pretences.'

Sarah turned back to the screen. 'Give him time, Jade,' she said. 'Tory's too good a businessman not to be able to work this one out for himself. Of course some of the trouble could come from the fact that he's not usually wrong in his character assessment.'

'Then you think he's right too!' Jade couldn't keep the disappointment from her voice.

'I didn't say that,' snapped Sarah irritably, annoyed that such a construction had been placed upon her words. 'And don't sit there all night with a long face, Jade, or I'll ... I'll box your ears! I told you yesterday, I don't like sour faces around me!'

With eyes widening in astonishment at Sarah's choice of chastisement, Jade found little difficulty in imagining the colonial McGraths expressing the same sentiments to their servants in days gone by—and carrying out the sentence—and the whole situation suddenly struck her as being so funny that she burst into laughter.

'That's better,' Sarah grudgingly approved. 'If you used that pretty smile of yours on Tory you might find him more amenable to your explanations,' she proposed with old-fashioned feminine logic. 'Why you young girls of today insist on equality and trying to beat a man at his own game, I don't know. We used to engage in a lot more interesting, and pleasing, ways to get our men around to our points of view when I was young.' She shook her head reprovingly. 'If he's any man at all he won't let a slip of a girl lock horns with him ... and win! And,' with a sly smile, 'if you're honest with yourself, you'd admit that you wouldn't want a man you could beat anyway!'

'I can't say that I altogether agree with you,' laughed Jade, 'especially not in regard to Tory. If I suddenly started smiling sweetly at him he'd only think it was his money I was after.'

'Who's after whose money?' came the lighthearted question as Barbara entered the room, eyes glowing, and proceeded to tuck her feet beneath her casually on the wine velvet couch.

'Tory's under the impression that Jade came out here with the idea of finding a wealthy husband,' Sarah explained drily.

'Ah-hah!' exclaimed Barbara in satisfaction. 'So that's why he was needling you in the dining room. I wondered what was going on.' She faced Jade inquisitively. 'And just how did he come upon that idea?' she asked.

'Because I *jokingly* said that was why I'd come out here when I met the men in the hotel last Saturday—and Tory overheard me,' Jade replied, flatly truthful.

'Strange,' was the thoughtful comment. 'It's not like Tory to be unable to take a joke with the best of them. Are you sure that's all it was?'

That there might be more than one reason—the reason that Tory had mentioned—had never occurred to Jade, and she stared at Barbara in no little consternation.

'Don't tell me there's more!' she joked mirthlessly. 'What else could I have possibly done? I'd never even spoken to Tory until I had my interview.'

'Oh, well, perhaps Laura had been giving him a hard time and that meant your "joke" didn't sit too well. Not that I'm surprised, mind you, Laura Emery would give anybody a pain.' Barbara evidently didn't like Laura Emery. 'Now there's a girl who would marry for possessions,' she went on, uncustomarily acid. 'How Tory puts up with her I don't know. I wish he'd send her packing.'

'That will do, Barbara,' Sarah spoke up sharply. 'The Emerys have been good friends of ours for many years and are always welcome guests in this house—as you well know.'

'And how!' Barbara rolled her eyes skywards, but at the disapproving look from Sarah conceded swiftly, 'Oh, her parents are okay, but Laura and that brother of hers are the living end. If Tory's not careful she'll successfully inveigle

80

him into marriage—something she's been after for years—
and then he'll see her true colours!' She wagged one forefinger in Jade's direction. 'I give you fair warning—watch
Laura Emery when Tory's not around, because she's like a
chameleon, she changes character to suit her surroundings.'

'Barbara!' Sarah interrupted more strongly this time,
catching her granddaughter with a brilliant gaze. 'I hardly
think Jade is interested in your version of Laura's short-
comings, nor do I think it's correct to talk about her in such
a fashion in her absence.'

'But, Sarah, you must admit that it's the truth,' Barbara
returned, unabashed by her grandmother's stricture and
waving a hand towards the girl seated in the next chair,
'and you couldn't allow Jade to come up against her un-
prepared. I mean to say, can't you just imagine Laura's
reaction when she finds someone with Jade's looks actually
living under the same roof as Tory?'

'Me?' Jade was astonished and didn't mind showing it.
'What have I got to do with it? Tory and I can't even have
a civil conversation with one another!'

With a delighted laugh Barbara recommended, 'Don't
sell yourself short! Laura's not blind,' another chuckle,
'and she's well aware that Tory isn't either! The only thing
I'm sorry about is that I won't be here to see the look on her
face when she discovers how young Sarah's new companion
is!'

'Don't talk such rubbish, Barbara,' Sarah now snorted
tersely, annoyed with herself for having allowed her granddaughter to go on at such length. 'Laura may not be perfect, but then neither is any one of us. She's a very polite
and thoughtful woman and I will not have you criticising a
frequent guest to this house in such a manner—do you hear
me?'

Barbara grinned sideways at Jade conspiratorially, but
managed to murmur in suitably dulcet tones to her grandmother, 'Yes, Sarah, I hear you, and I couldn't agree with

81

you more. Laura is polite and thoughtful ... when it suits her,' she couldn't help adding incorrigibly.

Remonstrating with her granddaughter wasn't having a very satisfying effect as far as Sarah was concerned, so she now changed on to an entirely different subject.

'I gather from your previous statement that you've prevailed upon Tory to fly you to Brisbane on Wednesday after all.'

'Verbally bludgeoned would be a more apt phrase than "prevailed upon", I think,' retorted Barbara with feeling. 'He was most reluctant to leave the property, but he's managed to extract his revenge by informing me that we'll be leaving at seven in the morning.' She looked round for support. 'I ask you, what sort of time is that to be leaving? I'm normally only just waking up by then.'

'As Tory already knows, only too well,' supplied a knowing Sarah. 'Perhaps that's his way of making sure you're ready to leave at a decent time instead of keeping him waiting around for an hour or more as you usually do.'

'Could be,' agreed Barbara nonchalantly, then grinned. 'But I'm not arguing with him about it. I was only too pleased when he finally agreed to take me. I didn't think he was going to at first.'

By ten o'clock Jade had seen Sarah upstairs to her room and then hurried along the gallery towards Helen's bedroom, intent on discussing their separate events of the day. However, Helen wasn't there, and after walking slowly back to her own room she noticed a small note placed prominently on her dressing table. As she had guessed, it was from Helen, saying that she'd waited until eight-thirty and then, as Mike had come across to see her, they had gone out, and she hoped that Jade didn't mind.

A smile teased the corners of Jade's mouth. Why should she mind? Mike seemed very nice and Helen was old enough to take care of herself. Besides, she couldn't expect her friend to sit around every evening on the off-chance that she might occasionally turn up.

Jade glanced at the small square-faced watch encircling her left wrist and sighed. It was too early for bed and she didn't feel ready for sleep yet anyway, so, after lighting a cigarette, she opened the doors on to the balcony and crossed over to lean her forearms against the pretty wrought-iron railing. Through the dense foliage of the surrounding trees she could just make out the lights shining from some of the station hands' cottages, and the lights from the rooms below her threw bold patterns on to the paving and the emerald lawn. There was a slight breeze blowing that ruffled tiny curls on her temples and a golden yellow moon that permitted her to espy in the distance some of the herd of Santa Gertrudis stud cattle owned by the McGraths, which were eagerly sought after in the cattle breeding industry.

Another sigh and Jade turned back to her bedroom, stubbed out her cigarette in the dainty leaf-like ashtray and made for the door. She was sure Sarah wouldn't mind if she borrowed a book from the library and perhaps, her steps quickened at the thought, she might even be able to find some mention of her ancestor. She knew a lot of the pioneer families had kept day books and records of rations purchased, handed out, and so forth, and with a library like the one downstairs surely it wasn't too much to expect that the McGraths still had in their keeping some of the original records.

With that idea still in mind, and a pleased smile on her face, Jade pushed the door open and came to a shocked standstill, her smile being replaced by a look of uneasy nervousness when she saw Tory seated on the couch, long legs stretched relaxedly before him and a weighty leather tome in his hands.

Knowing herself to be colouring under his slightly questioning regard Jade mumbled a hurried, 'Sorry,' turned on her heel and pulled the door closed again behind her.

She thought she might have heard him call her name, but she wasn't waiting to confirm the fact and with hasty steps she rushed back to the stairs. However, only one foot had made it to the first carpeted tread before her arm was caught in a firm hold and she was swung around to face a Tory who wasn't prepared to let her go so easily. At the humorous expression on his face Jade felt the muscles in her legs begin to wilt and she wished with all her heart that she could sink down on to the stairs only a few feet away. Instead she looked pointedly at the hand still capturing her arm, then haughtily eyed the man beside her.

That Tory didn't intend to release her was plain and his eyes outmatched her by making her lower her own to the region of the top button of his open-necked shirt, where she was left with the view of a sun-bronzed column of throat.

'Well, what were you after? Not me, that's obvious,' he laughed down at her softly.

Jade refused to meet his gaze, only shifting restlessly from one foot to the other and finally muttering, 'Nothing,' in a defiant tone.

A strong hand ensnared her chin, tipping her head back so that she had no choice but to encounter those very grey discerning eyes that were watching her so closely.

'You do like to live dangerously, don't you, Jade?' he tormented with a lazy smile. 'If you want a book—and I presume that was the reason you came to the library—then say so. Which one did you want?'

The warmth of that hand against her soft skin was having a calamitous effect upon Jade's senses, sending tingling shivers down her back and making her wholly conscious of Tory's vital masculinity in a way she would never have believed possible. Angry with herself for so willingly succumbing to an innate charm, she pulled her head away petulantly from his contact.

'What else would a girl like me want to read,' she

mocked carelessly, a bitter-sweet smile on her lips, 'but *Who's Who* or the *Social Register*? I mean, I really wouldn't like to miss *any* opportunity that might present itself when your guests begin arriving. A girl can't be too careful, and it's always a wise course to bone up on any prospective victim's background first,' she told him airily.

Jade almost expected to be flayed alive after that blatant summary of her imaginary intentions, but when no verbal attack was forthcoming she chanced a covert look from beneath dark lashes and found his return scrutiny was cool and guarded, leaving her no indication as to what he was really thinking. Now he merely waved one hand towards the open doorway.

'Be my guest,' he offered, casually indifferent. 'I'll get it down for you.'

No sooner had the words left his lips than once again he was tugging her along behind him until they came to stand by the shelves on the right-hand side of the library. Releasing her wrist at last, Tory reached to a shelf far above Jade's head, extracted a thick volume from among its neighbours and placed it in her nerveless hands. Jade glanced down at its scarlet cover in dismay. Now what was she going to do with it? She really didn't think it was the type of book that one took to bed to enjoy before going to sleep, and it certainly wasn't one that she had the slightest desire to peruse. But she had to say something—Tory would clearly expect her to make some comment—and she swallowed hard before making herself smile up at him gratefully.

'Oh, thank you,' she enthused with a studied gaiety. 'I'm glad to see you have the latest edition—I wouldn't want to miss anyone out.' She started edging back to the door. 'I'll have to get my notebook and ballpoint out and make some notes. It wouldn't do for me to forget any of the more important facts at a crucial moment, would it?' she dared to ask as she made it across the room.

'Like . . . who owns the most, and who's worth the most?' Tory surmised chillingly.

Jade held her breath fearfully but managed to open her eyes wide.

'Of course!' she endorsed in well-simulated surprise. 'What else?' and was around the corner and racing for the stairs before he could attempt any form of retaliation.

In the safety of her own room Jade showered and slipped into her pyjamas before sliding down into the more than comfortable bed. She rested back against the pillows and looked at the book she had left on the bedside table. Oh, well, she shrugged, it was still the only reading matter she had available, and picking up the work she propped it against her upraised knees.

An hour later and her eyelids were drooping wearily as she replaced the volume on the table and turned out the bed-lamp. That book really did contain a quite astonishing amount of information, she mused, as her head sank deeper into the pillow. She had recalled a few of the names of Barbara's intended guests and, more out of curiosity than anything else—but certainly not for the reason that Tory suspected—she had looked them up. By far the most impressive revelations had concerned the McGraths themselves. Was Tory really a director of so many companies? But for some incalculable reason she had been pleased to note that the Emerys had hardly rated a mention, and with this agreeable thought in mind she fell asleep.

CHAPTER FIVE

BEFORE Jade had a chance to dress the next day, Helen came rushing into her room and curled up on the end of the bed while Jade sorted through her wardrobe deciding what to wear.

'I haven't much time because I've got to be downstairs in a minute,' Helen began breathlessly. 'But I wanted to have a word with you and see how things went yesterday.'

Jade withdrew a pair of russet-coloured slacks, pulled them on, and made a see-saw motion with one hand.

'So-so,' she commented with a rueful grin. 'Sarah's okay, but that Tory—well, he's something else! Do you know,' she could laugh about it now, although it hadn't struck her as being the smallest bit funny at the time, 'he even dared to threaten to spank me yesterday?'

'He did *what*? Oh, he didn't!' Helen couldn't help herself and lay flat on her back, laughing. 'Now that is something I'd like to see. He doesn't know what he'd be taking on.'

'It's all very well for you to laugh,' Jade glowered back at her friend mock-ferociously, rubbing a meditative hand across the seat of her pants, 'but by the size of him I'd say he'd pack a pretty mean wallop!'

Helen sat up and wiped a hand across her eyes. 'I'm sorry I laughed, Jade,' she apologised, though quite unable to stop smiling. 'Whatever did you do to make him say that?'

'Oh, we were just having another of our scrimmages,' came the muffled reply as Jade pulled a close-fitting white top over her head. 'They seem to be becoming quite a regular thing.' She made an expressive face. 'I can even see

87

it getting to the stage where I shall miss them when it comes time for us to leave.'

Her friend's face sobered abruptly. 'Jade, I'm so sorry it's turned out the way it has for you. Are you sure you couldn't break that contract?'

'What? And have you languishing after Mike Johnson for the rest of the trip! No fear!' Jade teased. 'Anyway, I've sort of promised myself that I'll somehow wreak the family vengeance on Tory McGrath yet,' she went on with a secretive twinkle in her eyes.

'Just make sure it doesn't backfire, that's all,' warned Helen with a grin as she slid from the bed and headed for the door. 'Now I must go or I'll be late. See you later ... I hope.'

Once Helen had gone Jade brushed her hair until it shone and coloured in her mouth with a pearly pink lipstick, then tucking her copy of *Who's Who* under her arm she slipped quietly down the stairs and into the library. With the aid of an accommodating stool she replaced the book in its allotted niche and dusted her hands together with satisfaction. That disposed of that!

It was still too early for breakfast, and deciding that it would mean extremely wet feet if she took a walk round the grounds, as the dew still lay heavily on the grass, she made for the office. With luck at this hour of the day Tory would be absent and the earlier she started on Barbara's invitations the earlier she would finish them.

More familiar with the manuscript now, she began to make great inroads into the remaining pile and by the time she went in to breakfast they were almost all completed. Barbara greeted her with a ready smile and as they were the only two to put in an appearance—Barbara informing Jade that Tory would have had his hours ago and that Sarah always took her breakfast in bed—the two of them shared a desultory conversation throughout the meal until Jade returned to the office.

The last few envelopes were completed very quickly, and having handed them over to a pleased Barbara and tidied as much of the office as she could, Jade found time on her hands owing to the fact that Sarah had still not arrived downstairs. So with a quick tread she hurried along to the library once more and shut the door behind her. Now should be a good time to have a thorough look for any preserved family records.

She discounted the shelves on the right-hand side because many of the volumes had dust-jackets—a relatively modern innovation—but concentrated on those shelves partially hidden by the door where the bindings were a lot more worn and faded. It was a slow process trying to decipher the titles of some, and she would dearly have loved to take others down to read, but she was determined to check all the shelves first. Most of them had been printed during the last century and they covered a great many subjects.

The *Dictionary of Dates and Universal Reference relating to All Ages and Nations* printed in 1853 she made a mental note to peruse at a later date, as well as *Thoughts on Self-Culture—Addressed to Women* which she thought might well be an amusing eye-opener. Then, of course, *Hints on Horsemanship, to a Nephew and Niece; or Common Sense and Common Errors in Common Riding* by one Colonel George Greenwood, late of the Second Life Guards, might be quite handy too, she decided with a smile. She moved further along the shelves to a group of old hard-bound notebooks, and taking the first one down read the fine writing on the front cover with an increasing excitement: *Day Book, Marandoo, 1824 to 1826.*

Jade took the book over to the table and laid it down before her carefully and then began turning over the fragile-looking pages. It was like going back in time to see entries such as, '*Hunting cattle 17 or 18 away, self went out but could not find them*' ... '*Fixed the barrel churn for Emily*'

... 'Dray bogged, obliged to leave it for the night' ... 'Engaged all day helping Woolcott put up his house', and there it was, a reference to her ancestor: 'Pascoe minding cattle on run' almost immediately followed by, 'Gave Pascoe his week's rations, 12 lb flour, 7 lb beef, some tee (tea?) and sugar'.

All at once the door opened, bringing Jade back to the twentieth century in a rush, and making her jump guiltily to slam the book closed as Sarah came slowly to the table.

'Ah, the Day Book,' Sarah nodded comprehendingly, looking over Jade's shoulder. 'Been reading about the exploits of other Pascoes, have you?'

'I—I did notice the name,' Jade stammered, cursing the betraying colour that rose to her cheeks, but not knowing whether she should tell Sarah of her full knowledge of Red's involvement with the McGrath family or not. 'I like to read about the pioneers,' she added almost aggressively.

'Umm.' Sarah moved away and sat down in her usual chair. 'That Pascoe had red hair too,' she said musingly, but her eyes weren't reflective, they were ranged on to Jade's face with a bright penetration. 'And young Caroline wrote in her diary at the time that he had unusually beautiful eyes—they were a clear jade green.'

Jade jumped nervously to her feet and walked back to the bookshelves, saying over her shoulder with only a slight tremor in her voice, 'Oh, goodness, did he? What a coincidence!'

'Is it?'

Slowly she replaced the book with its contemporaries before turning to Sarah, a carefully blank expression on her face.

'Is it what?' she asked, deliberately obtuse.

'Jade!' Sarah's voice held a censuring sharpness. 'One of the reasons I gave you this job was because I believed you to be honest. Don't give me cause to regret that decision. There's nothing to be ashamed of in having a convict in

90

your family tree.' She chuckled quietly. 'Some of our best families have ... and we nearly did have.'

Jade's chin lifted a little higher. 'I'm not ashamed of it,' she retorted forcefully. 'I couldn't care less what Red did, I ... just...,' she broke off in confusion at the gratified look which spread over Sarah's face and shook her head wonderingly.

'You just ... what?' Sarah patted the velvet footstool beside her chair invitingly. 'Come here and tell me what's happened to the Pascoes since those days. I've often wondered.'

Seated on the footstool, her arms hugging her upraised knees, Jade smiled ruefully.

'There's not much to tell,' she said shyly. 'I gather Jane Pascoe married again once she reached Sydney, although her son never changed his surname, but I believe it was quite a litany of hate against the McGraths that she passed on to him. He's supposed to have grown up as rather a bitter young man.'

'Which doesn't surprise me in the least when one considers that it was Jane Palmer who raised him. Why, even Emily, Nathaniel's wife, who seems to have been a most soft-hearted and forgiving woman, wrote of her as a "flighty and troublesome piece",' Sarah interjected disgustedly, and at Jade's frown over the change of name, 'Oh, no, Jane Palmer was never a Pascoe, even though she might have called herself one, and she wasn't William's mother. She was only Emily's scullery maid. Mary Brinkley, the housemaid, was Red's wife and William's mother, but she unfortunately died soon after the baby was born and Jane Palmer used to look after the child while Red was out on the run all day.'

At least that explained the reason for Caroline wanting to elope with a married man—he hadn't been married at all at the time—but it didn't explain why Jane had been forced to leave the property and why she had saddled herself with a child that wasn't even hers, and Jade questioned Sarah on these points.

'Jane was given her notice to quit because it was found she'd stolen some of Emily's jewellery and sold it to a passing hawker. As for taking the child ... Caroline had dearly wanted to raise young William after Red had gone, but Jane had always made it clear that she wanted to be the second Mrs Pascoe, and it was generally believed that she took the baby in spite against Caroline, whom she considered to have taken Red away from her.' Sarah looked down at Jade inquiringly. 'You did know that Red was drowned, didn't you?'

'Yes, I knew that,' assented Jade. 'When he and Caroline were eloping together.' One eyebrow rose impudently. 'I gather that the McGraths weren't too enthusiastic about having an ex-convict join their ranks,' she laughed at Sarah.

'*Touché*,' admitted the older woman drily. 'But there could have been extenuating circumstances. Arrangements had already been made for Caroline to marry the elder son of another family. If the properties had merged then they could have become quite powerful, but even after Red died Caroline refused to marry her other suitor, and she remained single for the rest of her life.'

Good for Caroline, saluted Jade, but on looking round the room and noting once more the expensive furnishings—while still remembering what she had read about the family the previous evening—she began to smile.

'The lack of that merger doesn't appear to have set the McGraths back very far,' she couldn't resist declaring.

Sarah's look made Jade wonder whether she had perhaps gone too far, but then an unwilling smile touched her face.

'Don't be too impertinent, young lady,' she advised gruffly, 'or I might still box your ears. You're well within my reach while you're on that stool,' but there was no sting in her words, only a brusque kind of indulgence.

'I'm sorry, Sarah,' Jade begged her forgiveness straight away and indicated the room with an implicit hand, 'but this is all very different to what I'm used to.'

'And you're dissatisfied with your mode of living?'

'Oh, no!' Jade was quick to disclaim the implication. 'I'm very happy with my life. I share a pleasant home with parents whom I love dearly, and I earn enough money to buy most of the things I want. I just meant that this was . . .' she shrugged helplessly, '*different*, that's all!'

Sarah's eyes half closed and her lips pursed thoughtfully.

'Tell me about your parents,' she now instructed. 'I know nothing of the present-day Pascoes other than what I know of yourself, and that's very little. I'm interested to find out more about the family that would seem to have such an unsettling effect on the McGraths—one way or another—whenever one of them chances to set foot on this property,' she pondered ironically, silver eyebrows winging in interrogation.

A husky murmur of repudiation and Jade swept her hair agitatedly back behind her ears. She didn't know that she altogether cared for that 'unsettling' reference.

'Once again, there's not much to tell really. My father's the head of the science department at the local high school and my mother is . . . well, she's a natural born homemaker, I suppose you'd call it. She likes nothing better than thinking of ways to make her family more comfortable.'

'No brothers or sisters?'

'No, I'm the only one—the last of this particular line.' She inclined a mischievous smile upwards. 'You'll be able to breathe a sigh of relief that there'll be no more Pascoes to perturb this family—one way or another—once I've left the property.'

'And I'll be able to breathe a sigh of relief when you stop making such frivolous statements.' Sarah sounded annoyed. 'Go and get my book again and read another chapter to me.

That should keep you occupied until luncheon is served,' she declared pungently.

And so it did, because more than once Jade was commanded to read more slowly and to stop gabbling—which she was sure she wasn't—but she surmised that Sarah might be losing her hearing a little, although she refused to admit it, and from then on she sounded her words a little slower and a little louder, which seemed to suit Sarah admirably, for there were no more complaints forthcoming.

Lunch seemed an almost endless battle of nerves for Jade after she discovered that Tory would be present, and she waited expectantly for him to make some comment regarding her choice of reading material the night before. To avoid that apparently constant speculative gaze she kept her eyes on her plate for the greater part of the meal and the only words she uttered were a 'Yes, please,' when Barbara asked if she would like the salt. It had a distinct resemblance to sitting in the lion's den when he was waiting to be fed, and she didn't like the feeling at all! It made her lose any appetite she might otherwise have had and frayed her emotions into a chaotic tangle.

When the meal was concluded and Sarah announced her intention of going upstairs for her daily rest, to Jade's dismay Barbara offered to see her grandmother to her room as there was something she wanted upstairs herself. With bated breath Jade heard Tory call after them.

'I take it you won't be needing Jade this afternoon? Because, if not, there's a sizeable pile of correspondence that still needs to be answered.'

'All right,' his grandmother agreed from the doorway with an oblique look. 'Just make sure the child's here on time for dinner tonight. You know how I like my meals at regular hours.'

Jade wasn't certain whether Sarah's reprimand had been meant for her or Tory, but without waiting to find out she sprang to her feet murmuring nervously, 'I'll wait for you in the office.'

Tory's immediate reply came with a mocking patience. 'Sit down, Jade, and stop looking as if your death knell had just sounded. I'm sure you'll manage to survive an afternoon in my company without suffering any lasting damage.'

She wasn't so sure, but she wasn't going to let him know that, because she felt that she was letting him have a quite ridiculous effect on her, and it was putting her at an extreme disadvantage. With an effort she made herself resume her seat and smile guilelessly.

'Goodness, you have relieved my mind. By that I take you to mean that should I suffer any damage, it will be— lucky me—only temporary?' Her eyebrows rose sardonically at the last.

'Whichever way you look at it, it won't be "lucky you" if you don't watch your step, honey! You are one of the most provoking little wretches that it's ever been my misfortune to meet.'

'Only "*one* of the most provoking",' Jade allowed her eyes to open wide and her mouth to droop with effective disappointment. 'Now that does upset me,' she propped her elbows on the table and rested her chin on her linked fingers with a tantalising smile. 'You see, I do so always like to be the *best*!'

Tory's laughter echoed round the high-ceilinged room.

'And I'm sure that with only a little practice you could become just that! But in the meantime, as I told you yesterday, you might have to be prepared to take half a dozen of the best before you reach the top of the class!' he reminded her with a lazy grin, making a move to leave the table.

Jade spun out of her chair and stalked for the doorway, her head held high, completely forgetting for the moment her annoying pose.

'And as *I* told *you* yesterday, you'd better not try!' she flung at him over her shoulder.

'Is that a challenge?' his drawling call floated through the intervening space.

Safely at the doorway, Jade turned back and lifted one shoulder nonchalantly.

'Take it as you like,' she ventured recklessly, but made sure she was speeding down the hall before he had a chance to take her words at face value.

Even so, before she had managed to pass through the ante-room and into the office a firm hand had slid beneath her long hair and adamantly grasped the nape of her neck. Jade went rigid. Now what had her unruly tongue got her into? Tory pushed open the office door with his free hand and pressed Jade inside before his grip loosened and he lowered his head to the vicinity of one small pink ear.

'Relax, honey,' he advised in smooth amused tones, his breath warm against Jade's flushed skin. 'I've too much work on my mind to be indulging in the pleasure of man-handling you at the moment!' He propelled her lightly in the direction of her own desk. 'Just sit yourself down, there's a good girl, while I sort these papers out, and ... no distractions, please?' he requested with an irresistible smile.

Jade shrugged herself on to her chair and snatched the cover from her typewriter. She felt faintly piqued, but really couldn't fathom why. Perhaps because she knew herself far from immune to that overwhelming maleness that Tory exuded, without any apparent effort on his behalf, whereas he could dispose of her as an unwanted nuisance without any second thoughts. She glared resentfully at the downbent head with its loosely curling dark hair as he sorted through the papers littering his desk.

'And I'm not *honey*!' she contradicted rebelliously in a low whisper.

Tory lifted his head slowly. 'That you're not,' he agreed evenly, his slate-coloured eyes dark and cool in his bronzed face. 'Honey is sweet; it melts on contact with warmth; and gives generously of itself, *with no thought of reward*, when mixed with other substances ... and none of those descriptions would accurately fit you, would they, Jade?' He tilted his head considerably. 'An untamed wildcat might be more appropriate in your case, hmm? One whose claws badly need drawing and, for preference, right back to here!' as he made a savage slicing gesture with his hand across his throat.

It was a strain for Jade to maintain her valiant glance of indifference and her face felt stiff with the effort, but she was determined not to let him know how much his words had hurt. Digging deep into her reserves of will-power, she smiled tightly.

'That was a prime example of redundancy that you just used,' she told him haughtily as if she had never been guilty of the same offence in her life. 'Having used the word "wildcat", which automatically implies undomesticated, the word "untamed" was completely superfluous!'

'As you said you always liked to be the best, perhaps I considered that only by the use of the two words would the terminology be strong enough to depict you faithfully,' Tory replied with chilling exactness, totally unchastened by Jade's facetious attempts to correct his wording, and bent back to his paperwork.

Again she was left staring at the top of a dark head, but this time wordlessly. It wasn't fair, she fumed inwardly, her hands clenching in her lap. He switched from fascinating appeal to disparaging scorn with the facile ease of a master of disguises, and it was like trying to solve a giant riddle for Jade to predict just what his next mood might be. As it was he had her nervous system jumping from one end of the scale to the other with never a moment's respite.

At last he brought his head up again, asked Jade to bring her notebook over and, once she was seated in front of his desk, began to dictate at a speed that Jade was only just able to accommodate without having to request a pause. Whether anger was the underlying reason for the increased speed, or whether it was due to the amount of work Tory wished to get through she wasn't given the chance to contemplate, except for a certain amount of amazement that the running of a cattle station should generate so much correspondence.

As the final letter was added to the ever-increasing pile, Tory said his last 'Yours faithfully' with a thankful sigh while Jade gratefully stretched cramped fingers.

'I think that's the lot, thanks, Jade,' he rounded off formally. 'If you could type those tomorrow,' a dry smile, 'without keeping Sarah waiting for any of her meals, of course, it would be appreciated. The business ones you can sign, but the personal ones you'd better let Sarah see in case she wants to add anything, and then she can sign those.'

Jade acknowledged his instructions with a nod and rising gracefully to her feet took the pile of letters that Tory handed to her and returned to her desk, only to turn back inquiringly when he spoke again.

'Oh, yes, there was one other thing. There's a section of the stud records that I wanted duplicated. There's no rush for them but it will save me having to remember it when I get back from Brisbane.' He pointed to the large grey steel filing cabinet. 'They're in the first folder, top drawer. If you'd like to bring them over I'll show you which part I want copied.'

Withdrawing the appropriate folder, Jade took it over to Tory's desk and stood next to him as he sifted through the detailed pages.

'This is it,' he explained, indicating with a square-tipped brown finger, 'from September last year through to the present month,' and he ran his finger down the records.

As she bent over to make sure she didn't mistake the correct passage her hair slid forward and curled silkily on to his shoulder, but before she could sweep it back Tory had

98

brushed it away impatiently and snapped, 'For God's sake, get rid of that damned hair, Jade! It's annoying!'

Jade jumped back as if she'd been bitten, her face burning with humiliation, and whispered, 'I'm sorry,' in a small voice.

Even her hair was wrong now! It wasn't as if she'd done it on purpose and if he'd given her half a chance she would have brushed it away herself. Evidently every single thing about her angered Tory McGrath, she thought resentfully.

With her bottom lip caught irresolutely between even white teeth, she withdrew the stud records and placed them on the side of her desk along with the rest of her work, and while still feeling the smart of Tory's complaint she automatically went through the motions of rolling paper and carbon into the typewriter. Her cheeks continued to scorch with a rosy glow and her eyes glimmered brightly within their dark-lashed frames, but when they chanced to meet Tory's steely-eyed gaze she swung her head away sharply, suddenly deeply engrossed in her shorthand, and allowing her *annoying* hair to spill forward like a shining silk curtain and so hide her face from view altogether. As far as she was concerned Tory could go to Brisbane and never come back! She began typing angrily.

A few minutes later Tory moved lithely from his chair, passed Jade's desk without so much as a glance, and left the room with a determined tread. Jade stopped typing, took a cigarette from the packet she'd left in the drawer the day before and lit it. She needed something to help her relax! It was a while before her colouring resumed its usual honey-toned hue and her pulse returned to normal, but in the meantime she had taken two rubber bands and dragged her hair back into two very controlled bunches behind her ears. Perhaps that would please him better!

But she was not given an occasion to find out, for Tory failed to return to the office that afternoon and Jade typed on in solitude, making sure she didn't keep the family waiting for their meal that night by leaving the office in plenty of time to wash and change into a cool green and white crepe tunic, draw her hair back sharply from her face into a severe knot, and knock on Sarah's door to see if there was anything she could help that lady with.

Unaccountably Jade awoke early on Wednesday while the air was still chilly, and the sun, which had only just broken cover on the horizon, hadn't yet had a chance to dispel all the hazy pink shadows with its clear golden light; even the birds hadn't begun their early morning chatter. Expelling a deep breath, she slid further down on her pillow, clasped her hands behind her head and lay absently staring at the ceiling while her thoughts dwelt disturbingly on the events of the previous evening.

Not that anything terribly startling had occurred, but rather the disturbance was caused through Jade's own reluctantly admitted knowledge that Tory McGrath was not only an extremely magnetic specimen of virile manhood, but that he was coming to have an almost overpowering effect upon her newly-restive emotions—an effect she was using every means at her disposal to fight. It was no use permitting herself to be attracted to a man like Tory—he was used to living in a world where private planes, lavish parties and expensively beautiful old houses were the rule rather than the exception, a world far removed from her more humble code of life. Besides, what could she expect to gain from letting her feelings run on unchecked? Only more pain and anguish—especially since he believed she had only applied for the position with a view to furthering her own ends. Although, sometimes, when he treated her to a display of teasing charm she had to resist fiercely all her natural impulses to forgo the role she had chosen to play— or the role he had chosen for her—and stop attempting to frustrate him at every turn.

Like last night, for instance ...

After seeing Sarah to her room Jade had returned to the kitchen and spent an enjoyable hour talking with Helen and watching interestedly as Jenny worked the dough that would stand overnight before being baked into delicious crusty loaves the following morning. Suddenly remembering that some of her clothes still needed a pressing after having been cramped in her cases, Jade had ascertained from Jenny that she might use the iron and had gone hurrying up the hall, intending to collect the necessary items from her room, but before she could reach the foot of the staircase she had cannoned forcibly into Tory as he was turning out of the small room leading to the office.

Two vital hands clasped her shoulders firmly to steady her on her feet, but when she would have pulled away they seemed disinclined to release her and she was compelled to stand disturbingly close.

'I hear this is the second time the McGraths have employed a member of your family,' he drawled sardonically.

Jade looked startled—that hadn't taken him long to find out—and she searched his face for some clue as to his feelings on the matter, but being unable to discern anything definite she held his gaze unblinkingly and replied with a defiant lifting of her head,

'That's right.'

Tory's fingers moved slowly along the curve of Jade's throat and came to rest with a deceptively light touch against her fragilely exposed jawline. He inclined his head slightly, mockingly.

'Well, see if you can cause a little less of a furore while *you're* here, hmm? I shouldn't like to have to use too drastic a means of curtailing your activities.'

'And just what does that mean?' demanded Jade indignantly, fighting the insidiously lethargic feeling his hands were producing.

'I am still your employer,' he reminded her succinctly, removing his hands from her all-too-receptive skin to rest

101

them lightly upon his own slim hips as he leant one broad shoulder indolently against the door jamb, 'and you are still answerable to me for your actions. Don't forget that, Jade.'

Now that he had removed those disconcerting hands Jade felt more able to think clearly and she challenged him without flinching.

'And if I do?' she queried, sweetly scornful. 'What then? Will you have me flogged as your ancestors no doubt had their recalcitrant servants?'

A coolly deliberate scrutiny followed this remark which had Jade dropping her eyes confusedly and seething with anger when she heard his ensuing laughter.

'I doubt that any man would order a punishment that could disfigure a skin as smooth as yours, honey. Not even in those days,' he informed her, subtly taunting. 'I'm sure they could have devised other methods for keeping a little jade like you in line.'

Determined not to rise to his designed baiting with the derogatory use of her name a second time, Jade eyed him back stubbornly.

'Such as?' she prompted belligerently.

An experienced glance travelled purposefully from the enticing features of her face to the curves of swelling breasts and the flare of lissom hips.

'Looking as you do, honey, I doubt whether you would have been allowed out of the master's bed long enough to cause any trouble,' he replied with a supremely male arrogance, watching with an amused curve to his mouth as the deep colour invaded the soft cheeks turned to him.

A small gasp of embarrassment escaped Jade involuntarily before she could stiffen her resolve not to let him have the last word—not this time anyway—and with a sarcastic lift to one eyebrow she inquired 'And is that how your family behaved with their servants? Or perhaps they still do,' she gibed rashly. 'Is that how you get your kicks, Tory? A slap and tickle with the maids on the back stairs?'

A wide tantalising smile was all she received in return for her attempts to provoke and a softly retorted, 'If it was, the outcome might prove interesting in this particular case,' as he eased himself from the wall to flick a long finger at the end of her dainty little nose, '... or didn't you know that the McGraths have always had a weakness for beautiful redheads?'

Jade wasn't sure whether to be flattered by his description or wary of any possible intention behind the words. That he considered her beautiful gave her much-battered morale a decided lift, but the idea of Tory and herself being anything other than antagonists was one to be dismissed out of hand. It would put her at too much of a disadvantage, and she already doubted her ability to withstand a determined onslaught of McGrath charm. With a backward step she gave a passably pert smile.

'But in my case I'm sure you'll manage to make an exception and control the family failing. After all, it would never do for one of the great McGraths to become involved with a gold-digging hussy like me, would it? Just think of the shame, the degradation, the sheer humiliation of it all!' she finished dramatically with a flourish of one hand.

Tory treated her to a hard appraisal from smoky eyes as he took a step forward which sent Jade spinning away to flatten herself against the wall when he would have passed her.

'You know something ...?' he queried with a questioning incline to the set of his dark head. 'You talk too much!'

And he had walked on down the hallway with that self-assured stride of his while Jade had sagged visibly against the supporting wall, her mind in a turmoil. His last remark had left her with nothing to say, so sure had she been that he would agree with her self-maligning comments, and, when he hadn't it had taken the wind from her sails ...

Suddenly she heard Barbara's laugh come floating up on the crystal clear air, followed by the sound of men's deeper voices, car doors shutting and the quiet purr of a car engine turning over. With a defeated movement she threw back the bedclothes, pulled on a light cotton housecoat and padded over in her bare feet to the windows, where she stood gazing at the fast-disappearing tailgate of a white station wagon as it rounded the trees at the side of the house on its way, she presumed, to the airstrip.

With hunched shoulders Jade turned back to the room and took a cigarette from the packet lying on her dressing table. Lighting it, she drew quickly and paced back to the bed—the thought flashing through her mind that she was smoking far more these days than she ever had in Melbourne—but she was too restless to sit down and the windows drew her irresistibly once more. Soon after her cigarette was finished another sound broke the stillness—a louder, more penetrating engine this time—and looking upwards through the glass she could see the red and white Cessna banking slightly as it half-circled the homestead before heading east and winging its way out of sight in the brilliantly blue sky.

CHAPTER SIX

ONCE she had overcome her surprise at Tory's not returning to the homestead as expected, the succeeding week
proved eventful and pleasurable for Jade. As usual she
spent her mornings with Sarah, of whom she was losing her
slight wariness as they discovered their mutual likes and
dislikes and enjoyed companionable hours exchanging family histories and discussing the beginnings of both families
in a strange new land.

Most afternoons, for at least a few hours, she assisted
Mike in the office while he deputised for the absent Tory,
but from then until dinner she usually had free time, during
which she had familiarised herself with the layout of the
outbuildings and cottages and had been introduced to the
remaining members of the staff.

Late one lazy afternoon as the shadows were lengthening
across the landscape, Sarah had forgone part of her rest in
order to show Jade over the faithfully preserved clay and
pine cottage that had been the original homestead with its
quarried fireplace, ceilings of white-washed canvas and
walls draped with calico, although the stringybark shingle
roof had now been replaced with iron. Inside, most of the
furniture had been immaculately maintained, and Jade
listened with avid interest as Sarah lovingly recounted the
background of each artefact that particularly arrested
Jade's attention, and explained how the present home had
begun as a neat little two-storeyed building of sandstone
taken from a nearby quarry and had been enlarged over the
years by each successive generation until it had become the
imposing residence of today.

Jade had also renewed her acquaintance with Gary and

had enjoyed some relaxing hours in his undemanding company. On Saturday night there had been a party at the Kearneys' cottage which most of the younger employees had attended and they had talked, laughed and danced their way into the early hours of Sunday morning.

But still there was no indication of Tory's returning, and more and more often during the days that followed Jade found her hand-shaded eyes turning skywards at the least little sound that even remotely resembled a plane engine, or, as often as not, at no sound at all. It was becoming an unconscious habit, she decided wryly.

Sarah wasn't very forthcoming about the reason for her grandson's protracted absence, only telling Jade that he had phoned to tell them that he had some business to attend to, and when she had tried to question Mike he had only laughed and explained that it was quite normal for Tory to get caught up with extra problems once he arrived in the city and that he would be back as soon as he could make it.

This hadn't exactly quelled Jade's feeling of restlessness and she spent many a long quiet moment pondering as to why she should care anyway! Admittedly she found Tory extremely attractive, but she hardly thought that was enough reason for her to be so down-hearted just because he was away. All in all, it wasn't a very satisfactory state of mind she was in. She perversely found herself hoping that when he did return he would renew his attack on her character and thus give her the opportunity of overcoming her feeling of attraction with one of dislike, or even indifference.

During Monday afternoon she had driven Sarah over to West Springs, a large country town some miles distant from Wayamba, boasting a great many more facilities and amenities than that tiny outpost, and while she left Sarah visiting some old friends Jade had an interesting couple of hours wandering round the town window-shopping and making a few necessary purchases.

Wednesday was heralded by a brief but heavy storm, and by lunch time everyone was complaining of the humidity and wishing for the hotter, but more bearable, dry heat of the previous few weeks. Once the meal was over Jade saw Sarah upstairs and then hurried to change into a pair of brief emerald green hipster shorts and a green and white check haltered midriff top. Tying her hair back into a swinging ponytail with a bright ribbon, she decided on the river as the coolest, most pleasant way to occupy herself for the afternoon, as Mike had informed her earlier that he would be out on the run all day and would not be requiring her capable services. With regret that, as Helen wasn't scheduled for time off too, she would have to make the best of her own company, Jade headed out of doors and down to the rushing waters of the silvery winding river.

The causeway, or crossing, as most of the hands called it, would be best for her purposes. Jade and Helen had been to the same spot a couple of times before since they had been told that, although the goldmining days of the area were long gone, people still amused themselves by looking for alluvial gold on the riverbed and among the rocks. Not that anyone had found any of commercial value, but when the river was flowing fast it was often possible to discover some new particles of the precious mineral that had been washed down from further upstream. Jade and Helen had only managed to pan a few grains from the river sand so far, but they had been pleased to uncover some very strikingly coloured pieces of stone which they thought might polish up nicely for pendant jewellery when they returned home.

From the edge of the causeway Jade looked down at the bubbling, clear water. It was rather a magnificent stretch of water downstream from where she was standing, as the river narrowed and deepened considerably while it foamed and surged around and over submerged and half-visible rocks for some half a mile before the banks widened again and it subsided into a quietly flowing stream once more.

Her sandals left on the bank and a floppy-brimmed sun-hat perched on her bright curls, Jade moved out into the water with her panning dish, relishing the cool swish around her ankles but noting that after the morning's shower the water was deeper than usual when she moved further out and it was very soon swirling around her knees. Bending over, she began her intent perusal of the stony bed. An hour later she scooped up a handful of water and splashed it over her face before coming upright with a re-signed sigh at her lack of discovery—not even a pretty stone today to show for her labours.

The almost exasperatedly spoken words, 'And just what the hell do you think you're doing?' had her whirling around so fast that she nearly lost her balance as she stared at the man seated on a shining black horse close to where she had left her footwear. For a moment Jade looked at him disbelievingly. She hadn't heard the plane and Tory was the last person she had expected to see, but after shaking her head as if to clear it, she found she couldn't dispute her vision and, what was more, he seemed to be even taller and broader than she remembered.

His face was shaded by the wide brim of the bush hat pushed well forward on his head, but she sensed that his penetrating eyes had never for one moment left her own face as he waited, now clearly impatient from the set of that wide mouth, for an answer to his question.

Jade couldn't help the provoking smile that sunnily lit her features, curving the corners of a soft mouth appeal-ingly, as she faced him with her hands lightly resting on the contours of a slender waist.

'Nothing more than you would expect of me,' she enun-ciated clearly. 'I'm searching for gold ... what else?'

108

'And didn't anyone tell you that this section of the river can be extremely dangerous?'

But nowhere near as dangerous as a run-in with you on dry ground, she advised herself. Aloud she replied confidently,

'Mike and Gary did say to be careful, but we've had no trouble so far, and it's not as if I can't swim.'

Tory heeled his mount nearer to the water's edge, moving slightly in the saddle and causing the sun to scythe brilliantly across the side of his face, throwing light where there had previously only been shadow. One eyebrow crooked sardonically towards the heaving currents only a few feet from where Jade was standing.

'I hardly think you've had much practice in waters like these.' His voice sharpened. 'I suggest you remove yourself immediately. We've already had one death on this crossing —we don't need another!'

A death! Jade looked downstream quickly, her eyes wide. No one had thought to mention that! And suddenly the idea came to her. Could that possibly be Red he was talking about? Was this where their dray had overturned that fateful night? No doubt they hadn't had many crossings to choose from in those days. She began to push through the river hurriedly, resolved to question Tory on this point in her family history, but she hadn't made it further than a couple of yards when her foot slipped on the mossy side of a stone and during the struggle to regain her balance her stumble took her closer to the side of the rock-built causeway. The next time she put her foot down firmly the slippery edged crumbled, pitching her sideways into the rushing water.

After the first stifled gasp of surprise Jade's first thought as she sank beneath the swirling cascade was that she should be able to swim across the current and reach the safety of the bank further downstream, but upon surfacing she found that even during that short period of time the flow had

109

already carried her among some sinister-looking rocks and she now had to concentrate all her efforts in an attempt just to keep her head above water. Normally she accounted herself a moderately strong swimmer but, as Tory had warned, in waters like these she began to discover that her swimming ability was of little use, and what was making it worse was the fact that she had lost her ribbon as well as her sunhat and her hair kept sweeping across her face, often blocking her sight completely.

Even so, it wasn't until she was thudded into a submerged rock, leaving one leg bruised and sore, that she began to fear for her life. She wasn't going to *drown* ... she was about to be battered to death! Now she was dragged under the maelstrom once more as the river savagely drove between two closely located rocks, with Jade's shoulder bearing the brunt of the collision as they passed. Again she emerged, trying to brush the hair from around her face as she did so, and frantically trying to escape from the main stream and reach the slightly less violent side currents. She had only just managed to make it around the next collection of granite obstacles when there loomed before her the roughest section of turbulence she had yet traversed, and with a sheer gasp of fear she felt herself twisted sideways and tumbled over and over beneath the water until she was sure her lungs would burst. Then amazingly she was breathing sweet air again, but not before she had been slammed into a rounded stone that protruded some six inches above the foam, the side of her face making a painful contact.

With a strength born of exhausted desperation Jade flung her arms around the rock, willing the river to desist pulling her from safety, while she coughed and choked the unwanted intake from her lungs and laid her head wearily against the rough surface. Suddenly something warm touched her shoulder and she gave a low scream, imagining that some indescribable denizen of the deep had come to claim what the rapids had lost, but too shaken to put up

110

anything more than a vocal resistance. She turned her head slowly and encountered an expression of undisguised relief on Tory's face as he brushed the waterlogged hair back from his own forehead, but it was soon replaced by a look of glittering anger.

'You irresponsible little fool...' he broke off savagely, obviously only just keeping his temper and taking a deep breath to steady himself. 'You could have had us both killed!'

Only too well did Jade know that now, but she could only gaze at him dumbly through the curtain of hair that was plastered slickly about her face, and something of her shock must have reached him, for his face softened relentingly and he brushed aside her clinging hair with a surprisingly gentle hand.

'That damned hair again,' he taunted with tolerant exasperation, but when he saw the scratches now revealed a frown of regret creased his wide forehead. 'C'mon,' he urged gruffly, placing a supporting arm around her waist and holding her close against his side. 'Let's get out of here.'

She threw an anxious arm of her own around Tory's neck, clinging to him tightly and bringing a faint wry smile to his lips as they made their slow and deliberate way from outcrop to outcrop until they had, at last, reached the calmer waters near the edge and Jade could feel solid earth beneath her feet again. Soon Tory had helped her from the river and she sank weakly down on to the grassy bank, shaking with reaction and clasping her hands together around her raised knees in an effort to avoid bursting into tears of relief. It had been a harrowing experience and not one she would care to repeat.

In a leisurely movement Tory lowered himself to the ground beside her and a firm hand settled on the nape of Jade's bowed neck. For a minute or so it rested there consolingly, then he tilted her head back and held it imprisoned while cool eyes surveyed the damage done to the smooth skin. Jade's eyelids fluttered down, closing out the sight of those disturbing features, and she put up a hand self-consciously to her painful cheekbone, feeling the bruised and grazed flesh beneath her fingers.

She heard Tory's voice as from a distance when he sighed quietly and said, 'I don't expect it will leave a scar.'

Jade raised eloquent eyes then to inquire, 'Would you care?' in a tone of doubting bitterness.

His softly affirmed, 'Yes, I'd care,' took her completely by surprise, but no more so than the ensuing sweetly lingering pressure when his shapely mouth caressed her softly trembling damp lips a moment later.

His kiss was only for a fleeting second, but Jade knew she had involuntarily responded and now she dropped her green gaze in confusion. Gone was the shaking reaction to her recent experience in the churning water, but in its place was a shattering upheaval of her innermost emotions that she fought hard to control. What was the matter with her that such a casual kiss could affect her so? Of course he'd care if her face was scarred. Why wouldn't he? He probably thought she'd sue the company for compensation or something similar!

But there had still been no reason for him to kiss her— even if it had been casually performed—and she could fathom no reason for his behaviour. Unless it had been in the nature of a kiss as given to a child to comfort and soothe, which, of course, it must have been. There could be no other possible reason for Tory to kiss her. After all, he'd told her often enough exactly what he thought of her!

To cover her bewilderment Jade now moved uneasily under his observation and stiltedly tried to bring a little levity into the situation.

'That stretch of water seems very handy for getting rid of unwanted Pascoes,' she laughed brokenly, nodding towards

112

the river. 'I presume it was Red's death you were referring to earlier?'

As if he had been following her mental processes Tory's lips twitched with a masculine amusement as his eyes roamed the still water-speckled face turned towards him.

'It was,' he supplied finally. 'But that was his own doing —not the McGraths'.' A teasing look entered his eyes. 'In your case I'm sure we would be able to devise some less violent method. As *you* like to be the best ... *we* like to be original,' he mocked.

Jade could well believe that, and she could also believe that Tory still wasn't reconciled to having had to employ her against his wishes. It wasn't a good feeling to know oneself hired only with reluctance, and inwardly she rebelled at the thought. Outwardly she replied impudently,

'What a pity for you that I came up with a condition of employment of my own, otherwise I'm sure you would have managed to find a reason to have me bundled off your property and out of your sight by now!'

To her utter amazement he laughed, showing startlingly white even teeth against his bronzed skin.

'If that was all I wanted, I could still do it,' he told her.

'But—but—the contract!' she reminded him uncertainly.

'Ah yes, the contract.' Tory smiled infuriatingly, taking his time before enlightening her. 'You really should read all of a contract before you sign it, Jade. It might give you protection from being fired,' he smiled again, mockingly, 'but it also gives me the right to transfer you to *any* property that the company owns for the term of your employment.'

'But I was hired as Sarah's companion! I could hardly fulfil that function anywhere but here, could I?'

She refused to allow him to see how his last piece of news had shaken her. Why, he could send her to the back of beyond for the next couple of months if it suited him, and

113

that certainly wasn't what she and Helen had on their itinerary!

'You were also employed for secretarial duties,' he reminded her. 'I'm sure I could persuade Sarah to my way of thinking if I told her your services were more urgently required elsewhere. Sarah's very company-minded if approached the right way.'

And you'd know the right way, of course, thought Jade bitterly, her mouth setting in mutinous lines.

'Do I have a choice of where I'm to go? Or have you already picked the most distant one out for me?' she flared at him heatedly.

'No.'

'No *what*?'

That annoying smile was back again as he informed her lazily, 'No—you do not have a choice. And no—I have not picked one out for you.'

'Well, where am I to go then?' she demanded to be told, anxious to find out the worst.

'Nowhere. If you have to be working for the company at all, I prefer to have you where I can keep you under surveillance myself.'

'But—but you just said . . .'

'No, I didn't,' he cut in, exasperatingly keeping the upper hand. 'I said the contract gave me the *right* to transfer you—your own impetuosity jumped to the conclusion that I *would*!'

Of all the contemptible . . . ! He'd deliberately led her to believe . . . ! Jade's breasts rose and fell sharply with her rapid breathing and she glared at him impotently. He'd thought his hand had itched to slap her—she could assure him it was as nothing compared to the desire she was now experiencing to raise her hand to him, but she managed to control her anger to the extent where she only curled her fingers tightly into two small facsimiles of punishing fists by her sides.

'That's better,' he commended with a thread of laughter apparent in his voice as if she had spoken her desires aloud. 'Or you might find yourself getting more than you bargain for.'

'And what's that supposed to mean?' she queried scornfully. 'That I would, as threatened, end up over your knee?'

'Or in my bed.'

Her face burning, Jade momentarily retreated from that deliberate piece of provocation and scrambled unsteadily to her feet. She wanted to retaliate with a pithy denunciation to Tory's suggestive comment, but couldn't formulate the words because of the images her mind was managing to conjure up before her eyes.

To her absolute self-disgust she found that the idea had a distinct appeal and she wondered if the shock of her discovery showed on her face when those grey eyes held her own almost hypnotically, even as she imagined that muscular body hard against her own and those competent hands caressing her warm skin...

A vigorous shake of her head dispelled the rest of Jade's provoking daydreams and she hurriedly began moving up the bank, only to stumble weakly after a few steps. She might have fallen had not a sustaining arm caught her firmly and steadied her. A breathlessness that wasn't normal overtook her and she pulled away from him agitatedly.

'I—I'm sorry to be such a nuisance,' she said as formally as she was able. 'I don't know what came over me—I'm not usually so clumsy.'

'You probably don't usually spend your afternoons half-drowning in rivers either,' was the dry reply.

'Or being told that I might be taken to bed in punishment for my sins,' she couldn't help adding with a little more spirit. 'As a child *sent* to bed, yes, but never *taken* to bed.'

It wasn't until she'd fully digested his satirical, 'Keeping yourself for that wealthy husband you mean to find, eh?

Very thoughtful of you,' that Jade realised the construction he'd chosen to put upon her comment and she strove for a mocking expression of her own.

'But of course,' she agreed sarcastically. 'For what I'll be costing him he's entitled to a first edition.' She turned innocent eyes on him. 'Don't you think so?'

With a gesture that could have been the beginning of a sharp retaliation, or the brushing away of an irritating insect, Tory moved one hand upwards and then changed his mind and thrust both hands deep into the back pockets of saturated drill pants to stand looking down upon Jade's still inquiringly upturned face.

'I think you could find yourself paying a high price for that particular piece of effrontery if we stay around here much longer,' he told her unequivocally. 'Perhaps it's just as well you stumbled—it served to remind me that you've undergone a rather nerve-racking time and you're not really capable of defending yourself—either verbally or physically—at the moment.'

'You think not?' essayed Jade daringly under her breath, more as a confidence booster to herself than as a challenge to her companion.

He apparently wasn't prepared to see it that way, for, with a dangerous glint in his eyes and an incredibly swift movement, he held Jade captive within the circle of unyielding arms and a firm immobilising hand was at the back of her neck. This time when his lips met hers the pressure wasn't light and comforting, it was potent and persistent, and after her first surprised acceptance she began to struggle hopelessly against the husky body whose virile warmth she could all too clearly feel through both sets of wet clothing. But there was to be no escape, for his mouth became more compelling and intoxicating until her lips surrendered beneath his with a sigh and her mouth clung with a mounting fever while her arms wound themselves across

116

those broad shoulders to tangle in the dark wet hair at the back of his head.

Abruptly she was turned loose, to stand bemusedly watching the tantalising gleam in the black-lashed eyes of the man before her.

'I think not,' he copied her own statement, and an eyebrow rose outrageously. 'You're not capable of defending yourself. At least—physically—you're not,' he drawled with a captivating smile that had Jade averting her eyes rapidly as her heart beat an erratic rhythm against her ribs.

In a kind of daze she allowed him to slide a supporting arm around the exposed skin of her waist, which did absolutely nothing to help restore her mental balance, as they began their ascent of the slope taking them away from the shining waters and back towards the homestead. All the time she was totally conscious of the powerful body so close beside her own and she tried to sort out her own dishevelled emotions.

Again his kiss had taken her completely unawares and she was shocked and humiliated by her own uninhibited response after her short and ineffectual bid for freedom. If she was honest with herself she had to confess that she could perhaps have made a stronger, more determined attempt to break free, although she doubted that it would have made much difference to the outcome against Tory's superior muscle-power, but it would have saved a little more of her own pride and self-respect, which had already suffered more than enough for one afternoon. To have returned his kiss with such abandon when she knew only too well how he regarded her had been not only foolish in the extreme but mortifying as well.

She stole a covert glance at him from under curling lashes—it wasn't as if he was the most attractive man she'd ever met—no, that was a lie, she judicially corrected herself immediately—he *was* that, but up until now she had never considered herself as a girl to be roused by mere physical

117

masculinity, and the thought that she could be, after all, disturbed her deeply, for she knew that if Tory had again taken her in his arms at that very moment, she could not have failed to reciprocate his persuasive kisses. And that brought a worried crease to her normally smooth brow.

'I was right both ways, it seems.'

Tory's words brought Jade out of her reverie with a perplexed look.

'Both ways?' she queried.

'I said you weren't capable of defending yourself, physically or ... verbally.' His mocking smile had her heart leaping to her throat. 'I think the first has already been proven beyond the shadow of a doubt, and as you haven't said a single word for the last five minutes I feel I can lay claim to a victory with regard to the second also.'

As he had all too successfully turned her attempted resistance into a dismal rout there was nothing she could do but mentally agree with him—no matter how reluctant she might be to admit it—but she steadfastly refused to say so and treated him to a disdainful sniff and a haughty lifting of her head. Once again, let him think what he liked—she had only to survive for three months and then she and Helen could happily go their own way with no overbearing Tory McGrath telling her what she could and could not do!

The long slow walk back to the house, which gave ample time for their clothes to dry, Jade had to acknowledge was made more interesting as Tory indicated the points of note along the way; the now disused quarry where the stone for the house and cottages had been excavated; the sandy hollow near the river where one of their assigned stockmen had been speared by marauding natives during the last century, and the old burial ground where the original McGrath pioneers and their daughter, Caroline, were interred, as well as Jade's own ancestor and the luckless stockman.

It was a pretty place, set beneath majestic trees that

threw a cooling shade like a gentle mantle over the grassed slope, and surrounded by a small white picket fence. In her explorations around the homestead Jade hadn't come across the tiny graveyard before and she vowed to return on her own later in her stay to inspect the carefully tended plot more closely. Somehow it pleased her to know that Caroline and Red were buried side by side—that what they had been denied in life might have been achieved in death.

At the rear of the house Tory turned Jade to face him and touched a finger lightly to her grazed cheek. Strangely it didn't hurt, it was softly tranquillising.

'I should tend to that and then have a rest for the remainder of the afternoon,' he advised.

'Are you going to?'

'Going to what?' he drawled. 'Tend your wounds? Or have a rest?'

Jade gave him an exasperated glance, flushing slightly.

'Have a rest, of course. I can look after myself.'

His eyebrows rose and his mouth tipped at the corners. 'That's debatable,' he taunted. 'But no, I do not intend to rest—I have a mount to find that was left somewhat abruptly at the crossing. Why?'

Now that he'd asked the question she began to wonder herself just why she'd mentioned it. She turned away, shoulders sagging dejectedly, anxious only to seek the solitude of her room.

'No reason. I—I just wondered, that's all,' was the most she could find in way of a return on the spur of the moment.

'Just make sure *you* rest,' Tory ordered with a grin, flicking a finger at her. 'We've some wealthy guests coming to dinner tonight and you want to be looking your best, don't you?'

Inexplicably that remark had the effect of grating unbearably on Jade's nerves, and she snapped, 'Oh, go to hell!' before stalking onwards to the fly-screened doorway.

What effect her words had on him she wasn't sure, but

119

she felt certain she sensed, rather than heard, him laughing behind her, and giving her temper full rein she slammed the door resoundingly shut behind her and headed for the stairs. The bang, however, brought forth a dark head around the kitchen door and Helen's look of inquiry turned to one of consternation as she stepped quickly into the hall-way.

'Whatever's happened to you? Did you fall down the stairs, or something?'

'Or something!' repeated Jade with a grin. 'I fell off the crossing.'

'*The crossing!*' Helen echoed in a horrified tone. 'Jade! You could have been drowned!'

'So I've already been told,' with a grimace. 'Not that I needed the information after traversing those rapids under my own steam.'

Helen's face lost some of its worried creases and a smile started to spread over her mouth.

'And from your expression I don't need to be a genius to guess who said it. I gather you already know Tory's back.'

'Uh-huh,' Jade nodded. 'It was Tory who came after me and fished me out.'

'And was he also the reason for the slammed door?' Helen hazarded a rueful guess.

Jade pulled another face and laughed. 'How very obser-vant of you! But tell me, when *did* he arrive back? I didn't hear the plane.'

'Just after lunch, and the reason you didn't hear the plane was because he apparently flew back with the Masons —I think that's the name Jenny said—and then drove over from their place.'

'What's the matter with his own aircraft?'

'Jenny said his brother, Reid, and his family would be flying in tomorrow, so he left it in Brisbane and came back with Mr Mason.' Helen grinned. 'Anything else you want to know?'

About to shake her head laughingly, Jade chanced upon a sudden recollection.

'Yes. Who are the guests that Tory said would be coming tonight? Do you know?'

'Sure do,' affirmed Helen with a wink and a rapid scrutiny of the passage in both directions. 'None other than Miss Laura Emery, the lord and master's long-term girlfriend, and her brother, as well as a few other friends who live hereabouts. Eight of them in all, I believe. Jenny and I have been rushing around furiously all afternoon getting everything prepared. Which reminds me,' she continued with a swift look over her shoulder, 'I must get back and give Jenny a hand—I can't leave her to finish it on her own.' She put her hand on the swing door. 'By the way, Mike and I are going over to Gwen and Ian's later this evening. Do you want to come?'

Jade shook her head regretfully at her friend's expectant glance, shrugging her shoulders.

'I'd better give it a miss this time, thanks, Helen. With guests here I don't know how the land lies with Sarah, and it will probably be wiser if I keep myself available. Some other time, perhaps.'

'Okay, we'll take a raincheck.'

Upstairs in her room Jade showered and washed her hair, dressed in a pair of pale lilac shorts and matching top, applied a cooling antiseptic cream to her cheek and then propped herself up on her pillows preparing to do as she had been told, and rest. However, she wasn't used to sleeping so early in the day and she turned and squirmed restlessly for half an hour before finally going outside on to the balcony where she stretched out on a padded lounger.

Through the delicate tracery of the wrought-iron railings she could just make out the forms of Tory and Mike talking in front of the machinery shed and Ian Kearney coming up to join them, then a moment later all three men moved out of sight around the corner of the building.

Tory's unexpected appearance set Jade musing over her eventful afternoon and, in turn, brought her to the undeniable conclusion that his attitude towards her definitely seemed to have undergone a change since his sojourn in Brisbane. Oh, there had been that comment about putting on her best face for his guests tonight, but there had been no sting or contempt in his words. Rather he had seemed to mention it more as a joke. Could it be that, at last, he was beginning to see reason and realised he might have mistaken her motives?

Logically she moved on to her next point—the guests that would be arriving—and more particularly Laura Emery, his—what had Helen called her?—'long-term' girlfriend. Did that mean it was one of those continual on/off affairs, or that Miss Emery was on the top of the list in the marriage stakes? She could well imagine that Tory could have his pick of partners any time he chose and that, having reached the age that he had without being married, he could prove to be a very slippery fish to land. Perhaps that was the reason Laura Emery was 'long-term'. Maybe she hadn't come up with the right bait yet—as Barbara had intimated.

Jade snorted disgustedly. What business was it of hers anyway? Tory McGrath and his friends were way out of her league and, no doubt, were well able to manage their own affairs without any mental intrusion from herself. She was employed as Sarah's companion and a part-time secretary, nothing else, and it would be better if she kept that singularly dampening thought to the forefront of her mind.

For dinner that evening she dressed with great care in an elegant emerald green long flowing skirt teamed with a pristine white sleeveless wrap-around blouse in a subtly shimmering material which tied on the right-hand side of her waist. She applied a slightly heavier covering of make-up than usual, which almost succeeded in camouflaging her grazed cheekbone, and caught her hair into generous curls on the top of her head—she hadn't missed Tory's 'that damned hair again' at the end of her precipitate swim. Besides, not only was it cooler that way but also more in keeping with the restrained image she had created for herself, especially with the old medallion nestling securely against her creamy skin within the alluring vee of her neckline.

Even before she had been along the gallery to Sarah's room, Jade had picked up the sound of high-powered motors approaching, then the closing of numerous car doors, followed by the sound of mixed voices talking and raised in laughter, and for the first time really disliked the thought of dining with the family that evening.

She had nothing in common with these people—their lifestyle was worlds away from her own. What would they know of having to put aside a little money each week in order to be able to buy one particular outfit? They could order a dozen in one day and not even count the cost.

Suddenly she caught sight of her reflection in the mirror and an irrepressible grin began to break. If you don't watch it, my girl, she told herself, you'll find yourself becoming sour with envy. So what if they had money—it was said it couldn't buy happiness. The grin really came into being now. Of course the lack of it wasn't a necessary requisite for making one happy either! She and Helen had thought it might be fun seeing how the other half lived—well, she was certainly doing that, so she might as well enjoy the experience while she could.

A few minutes later when Jade entered Sarah's extremely feminine pink and white bedroom she found that lady had also been to a lot of trouble for their guests, being attired in a very becoming silk dress of lavender and silver that softly enhanced her still youthful skin. Around her throat she wore a strand of perfectly matched lustrous pearls that took Jade's breath away. No cultured pearls those!

Sarah ran her eyes approvingly over her young com-

123

panion's clothes, but as they came to rest on her lightly flushed features her eyes narrowed discerningly.

'What have you done to your face?' she demanded with a frown.

It only took Jade a few moments to explain—carefully omitting some of the not-so-relevant details from the narration, of course. Those she didn't care to relate!

'As if one Pascoe drowning there wasn't enough!' reprimanded Sarah brusquely, raising one small bony hand and tapping Jade softly on her unmarked cheek. 'It's a crime to mar a thing of beauty—be it a view of the countryside, a work of art, or a young girl's face. You have a beautiful face, Jade, and it gives people pleasure to look at you. Take better care of it in future.'

The face under discussion promptly burned scarlet—Jade still wasn't altogether used to Sarah's outspokenness—and to cover her embarrassment she laughed nervously.

'Is that a roundabout way of letting me know my looks are the only thing I have to recommend me?' she asked in a self-conscious attempt to ease away Sarah's extreme compliment, but the other woman took her seriously.

'Don't be ridiculous, girl!' Sarah quickly reverted to her old browbeating manner. 'I'm not such an old fool that I don't know there's an intelligent mind in that head of yours, or that there's a kind and thoughtful heart inside that very female figure either! A lack of vanity is very pleasant to see, but to hear you talk one would think that no one has ever called you beautiful before—and that I can't believe,' she stated dogmatically, and Jade thought it wisest to let the matter rest there before Sarah had a chance to become really warmed to the subject.

When they finally made their way into the already occupied drawing room it seemed to Jade as though they were approaching a sea of faces as everyone turned to watch them. Instinctively her eyes sought out Tory's commanding figure, standing at least a head taller than any other man in the room, as if seeking his approval—of what, she didn't know—but his glance was quite bland when she encountered it and gave absolutely nothing away. With a fractional lift of her chin Jade turned away and gave her attention wholeheartedly to Sarah's introductions, pleased when they were completed and she could study the group at length from her position next to Sarah while sipping absently from the glass of sherry that Tory had handed her.

In many respects there was a sameness about all of them; the fashionable and obviously expensive clothes; the polish and sophistication; and the almost tangible self-assurance. But once it came down to individual personalities the similarity ended.

It was only natural, or so Jade persuaded herself, that Laura Emery should be the subject of her first scrutiny. She was an extremely tall girl in her late twenties and, unfortunately, only slightly built, which would have given her the appearance of being angular had her stunning sapphire blue silk dress been not quite so expertly fashioned, while her careful make-up and elaborately coiffured blonde hair deliberately drew attention to her face rather than her figure. The wide mascaraed eyes were an uncomfortably penetrating shade of pale blue—a feature, Jade noted, that Laura shared with her brother, Elliott—and the wide brightly carmined mouth had turned down superciliously at the corners when they had been introduced, making it abundantly clear—to Jade at least—that Laura considered Sarah's new companion to be well and truly beneath her dignity to acknowledge as a fitting individual to join their élite circle.

Not so her brother, however—only a year or so younger than his sister but with the same tall thin build—for he carried an open invitation in his pale eyes that Jade found not only repellent, but faintly offensive as well. Quickly she brought her gaze round to the rest of the company.

Ann and Edward Mason were a vivacious couple whom

she warmed to immediately. At the moment Ann's dark eyes were twinkling merrily as she recalled her young daughter's latest escapade, the outcome of which had them all breaking into laughter—all, that was, except Laura, who only allowed herself a small conventional curve of thinned lips while her eyes remained icily pale. Evidently Laura was not the least bit interested in the exploits of little Gail Mason, making Jade doubt whether Laura even liked children at all. She didn't give the impression of being the type who could find any enjoyment whatever in spending her days with a smudged-faced, sticky-fingered, inquisitive-minded little miniature of herself, or her husband.

The other two couples, the Waldens and the Rickards, would have been in their late thirties and although their children were now past the toddler stage, it was obvious from their ready smiles that it hadn't been too long ago that they also had been experiencing the same sort of mischief that Gail had been up to that afternoon.

Jade sipped the last of her sherry, placed the empty glass upon a nearby table and a few moments later found herself tailing the others, with Elliott hovering close at hand, as Tory escorted his grandmother into the dining room. Taking her customary seat next to Sarah, she noticed with a sinking heart that Elliott had been placed on her other side, and before the first course had even been laid before them he had gravitated towards Jade and leant insufferably close.

Out of the blue he suddenly exclaimed, 'I know who you are!' loud enough for everyone at the table to hear, his insolent blue eyes raking over her intolerably. 'I thought I knew your face! You're the girl in that advertisement on television—the one wearing next to nothing and enticing all those men down on to the beach.' He laughed raucously. 'I bet you had fun filming those scenes!'

An enveloping fire consumed Jade, partly caused by the embarrassment of knowing that Elliott had spoken loud enough to draw the interested attention of the whole party, and partly from her own rapidly escalating temper. *Enticing!* She cculdn't believe that was how he really interpreted the ad. It had been filmed on the beach for the sun, the sand, and the sea—what could be more symbolic of good clean wholesome fun? It was a soft drink she had been helping to advertise, not a fillip for a man's sexual appetite as he was trying to insinuate.

Laura's disparaging, 'Oh, T.V. What else could you expect?' hit Jade's quivering nerves dead-centre and with a deeply drawn breath she faced Elliott squarely.

'If it had been as suggestive as you're trying to imply, I hardly think it would have managed to pass the Censorship Board. And, for your information,' she tried to smile naturally but couldn't keep all of the scorn from her eyes, 'it was supposed to be a beach party—not a midnight orgy—which explains the reason for my perfectly adequate bikini. One which, I might add, I've worn to the beach many times before and plan to wear again in the future.' This time she didn't even bother to try and keep the disdain from her voice. 'And I've never yet been chipped by a beach inspector because it was too brief!'

'Probably too busy enjoying the scenery,' laughed Ted Mason in the pause that followed her heated words.

With her temper really flaming by now, Jade's head spun to intercept Ted's gaze, another hot retort on her lips—she was damned if she was going to let these over-endowed members of the squatocracy use her as their target for entertainment—but as she saw his easy-going appreciative smile her wrath faded ruefully and she realised that he had meant his remark as a compliment and not as a gibe.

Amidst the general laughter that circled the table Laura's voice sounded a trifle high and forced.

'Oh, well, I suppose some girls do actually *like* bikinis,' she purred condescendingly, still managing to convey the idea that she considered it was blatantly evident just why they did.

127

In reciprocation Jade accompanied her honeyed assent of, 'Umm, *some* of us certainly do,' with a slow appraisal from Laura's head down as far as the table would allow and back up again, letting her own eyes leave the older girl in no doubt as to her silent thoughts. If she had a figure like Laura's *she* wouldn't wear one either.

Laura hadn't missed the almost insolent scrutiny, for a darkening pink found its way into her cheeks which had the effect of making her eyes appear even paler as they glittered vindictively across the snowy-white linen. If Laura hadn't been an enemy before, she certainly was now! But at least it had put an end to the sweetly caustic badinage, and for this Jade was duly thankful as the conversation returned to more general topics. It wasn't until they were half-way through their dessert—a delicious concoction of cherries, meringue and cream—that Elliott spoke directly to her again.

'I hope you'll believe me when I say I'm sorry for what happened before,' he murmured in what he clearly thought to be persuasive tones, sliding a warm clammy hand over Jade's own as it rested unsuspectingly in her lap. 'To make amends how about letting me show you the garden in the moonlight?' he suggested more confidently when there was no evidence of her removing her hand from his clasp.

Little did he know it, but the reason for Jade's stillness had been shock—not compliance! After his initial insinuations, coupled with his questing hand and overly bold eyes, no girl in her right mind would take on Elliott Emery in a deserted garden at night! And Jade was very much in her right mind.

With a tiny smile of politeness—it was really all she could rally—Jade extricated her hand from his, but before she could find her voice and decline the undesirable invitation Tory spoke from the other end of the table.

'Why don't you take Jade down and show her the museum, Elliott? She might like to see the old photos of the

128

gold nuggets they found in the river during the days of the rushes.' With a taunting smile he added, 'Jade's very fond of gold-digging . . . aren't you, Jade?'

Of course the first words Tory directed to her that evening would have to be along those lines and at such a moment! She should have known! But if he thought he was going to obtain his revenge by pushing her into Elliott's repulsive clutches, he could think again!

'Sarah's already shown them to me, thank you, Tory,' she had pleasure in being able to smile demurely at him, absently fingering the medallion round her neck. 'And I've already begun my own collection.'

Another smile, but this brought no response other than an imperceptible narrowing of Tory's eyes and a tightening of his lips, a fact which Jade noted with a glow of triumph, knowing that she had for once come out on top.

'Surely you can't have seen everything,' cajoled Elliott in disappointed tones. 'There must be some things you haven't inspected. I know the old place pretty well.'

'But not as well as I do,' put in Sarah challengingly, her blue eyes piercing as they pinpointed the young man. 'Besides, Jade happens to be *my* companion,' a brief victorious smile for Tory, 'and I shall be needing her this evening, so you can forget about any hand-holding in the moonlight, Elliott Emery. I haven't been feeling too well of late and I may wish to retire early tonight.'

At these words both Jade and Tory glanced at Sarah in some surprise—she'd never mentioned feeling unwell—but Tory took her defiant look head-on until an unmistakable gleam of recognition shone in slate-grey eyes. Sarah was siding with her young employee—a cat defending her kitten. Not that Tory seemed one whit put out by the disclosure, conceded Jade ruefully. He probably considered the disposal of a pair no more difficult than one.

But as they were adjourning to the drawing room for their coffee and under cover of the various condolences regarding Sarah's health from the other guests, Tory gripped Jade's upper arm tightly, staying her footsteps when she would have followed the rest into the hallway. He swung her around forcibly to face him.

'Started on your own collection, have you, Jade?' were his first taut words. 'What have you persuaded Sarah into giving you now? First a job—now what ... *this*?' and his free hand caught her medallion into his palm, pulling the chain tight round her neck.

Jade rallied quickly after her momentary stunned surprise.

'No! I did not!' she rejected his accusation hotly, her head coming up automatically to his in an attempt to relieve the pressure on the chain. 'And I didn't persuade Sarah to hire me either! She believed what I had to say at the interview.'

'I never doubted that for one moment. But if Sarah didn't give you the medallion ... where did you get it?'

She noted that he said 'Where did you get it?' and not, 'Who gave it to you?' Must he always be thinking the worst of her? Was he never to take her on trust? It was perfectly clear he was confusing her piece of jewellery with something else, and she wondered why it should seem so important to him. She expelled her breath on a sigh.

'My father gave it to me,' she replied at last.

His hand opened a fraction to enable him to inspect the delicate detail of the arabesque on the obverse of the golden disc as it lay shining against his tanned skin, then just as quickly his fingers folded over it once more.

'I can't accept that, Jade,' he bit out tersely. 'Your father never bought that for you—that's a piece of McGrath jewellery!'

'Not any more it isn't,' she couldn't help provoking in a low murmur.

Now a hard hand gripped her chin, forcing her head upwards so that she had no option but to meet his flint-like gaze.

130

'So ... Sarah did give it to you. Why lie about it? Did you honestly think I wouldn't find out?'

'I didn't lie—Sarah didn't give it to me.' She glanced at him through the thickness of her lashes and refused to resist the temptation to test the rein on his temper to the full. 'It was donated by a completely different McGrath.'

'Donated by a ...' Tory abruptly let go of her chin and the medallion, but his two hands came to rest forcefully upon her shoulders. 'If you don't stop the double-talk, honey, make no mistake, you'll get the biggest shaking you've ever had in your life. Now *give* ... whose medallion is it?'

'Mine,' Jade baited him incorrigibly, but on seeing his expression, 'Oh, all right, if you must know ... it was Caroline,' and at his uncomprehending frown, 'Caroline McGrath ... she gave it to Red Pascoe. See...' and she picked up the small piece of metal herself this time to show him the inscription on the reverse.

For a moment Tory bent to inspect the engraving and then he straightened slowly, his eyes lifting to Jade's with a wry apology in their grey depths.

'So there was another one. We'd always believed that there was, but had never been able to find it. I'm sorry I accused you of duping Sarah,' he said in all seriousness, 'but she has one exactly the same, only with the initials reversed, that Red gave to Caroline. Apparently they were a matching pair,' he enlightened her.

Now Jade could understand the importance he had attributed to her small decoration and impulsively she raised her hands to the tiny clasp and removed the chain altogether.

'In that case perhaps they should stay together,' she suggested, holding the keepsake towards him.

He smiled at her sentimental gesture but shook his head negatively.

'No, that one belongs to your family as much as its mate

belongs to mine. And what's more,' his eyes gleamed audaciously, 'yours enjoys a far more appealing setting than Sarah's. Hers only rests on a bed of velvet.'

Jade's cheeks flamed at this thought-provoking statement and the look in his eyes had her swallowing nervously in an effort to check the runaway ideas that skipped through her mind. To cover her discomposure she swiftly bent her head and occupied her hands with the task of returning the medallion to its original position.

'Tory! Do hurry up, darling. The coffee will be getting cold,' lilted Laura's voice from the direction of the drawing-room. Jade sighed gratefully at the interruption which saved her from having to reply to Tory's unabashed comment.

At the same time she had to lift a sardonic eyebrow at Laura's endearment, which earned her an intimidating look that sent her swishing past Tory and into the drawing room before he had a chance to fulfil the silent threat.

For the remainder of the evening Jade's time was divided between enjoyably chatting with Ann Mason or Marion Rickards, and repulsing Elliott's unwanted advances, until her head began to ache intolerably with the effort of retaining even some slight civility in her replies.

'Suppose I call for you early tomorrow and we can take a picnic lunch to a nice little spot I know down on the river?' he was trying to persuade her now, even while his eyes devoured every inch of exposed skin with an eager familiarity.

For the umpteenth time Jade shook her head wearily. 'I'm sorry, Elliott, but I'm not a guest here—I don't have any time off tomorrow. As you know, Tory's brother and his family will be arriving and I just can't see myself having any free time at all. Some other day—maybe,' she attempted to satisfy him.

But Elliott wasn't going to be put off so easily. 'Well,

when *do* you have your day off?' he demanded to be told precisely.

With a wry grimace Jade wondered why Elliott Emery had never learnt to accept defeat gracefully, or did he really believe that his money entitled him to act as one of God's irresistible gifts to women?

'When neither Sarah nor Tory needs my services . . . and it isn't often that those two circumstances conjoin,' she added for good measure. 'I usually get a couple of hours here, or an hour or so there . . .' she purposely sounded vague, 'and I never really know when it's going to be, so I can't tell until only a few moments beforehand,' she concluded breezily.

'But that's no way to treat an employee. I'll have a word with Tory before I leave and see if we can't come to some suitable arrangement to enable you to have some time with me tomorrow.'

Of all the nerve! Anyone would think he was interested in her working conditions, instead of worrying about his own nefarious plans. Why couldn't he just mind his own business and leave her alone? She could well imagine what Tory's reaction would be if Elliott hinted that she wasn't satisfied with the hours she worked. It would take a bit of circumvention to get out of this one.

Eyes lowered—they had to be or Elliott would have seen the absolute fury blazing out of them—Jade, convincingly nervous, twisted her hands together uneasily.

'Oh, no, please don't do that,' she pleaded softly. 'Tory might think I didn't want the position, or worse still . . . he might even fire me,' she continued, breathily eloquent, guessing that Elliott knew nothing of her contract.

'But it's not fair,' he exclaimed childishly at having his plans thwarted so effectively. 'How else am I ever going to get to see you?'

A sudden idea came to mind. 'Perhaps I could telephone

133

you,' she proposed helpfully. 'Some time when I know I'll be free for a while.'

Which, of course, would be never. Nothing on earth would persuade her to ring him and suggest a meeting, but he wasn't to know that and with luck he would tire of waiting for her and find some other poor girl to pester.

Finally Elliott conceded—albeit unwillingly—that this course of action appeared to be the only one left to them in the circumstances, and, with what Jade deduced was supposed to be a consoling smile for her loss of his exhilarating company, he eventually left her alone with Sarah on the sofa.

Hardly had she had time to sink back exhaustedly when Sarah leaned towards her asking if she would help her up the stairs as she was feeling tired, and with pleasure at not having to suffer any more of Elliott's attentions, Jade rose swiftly and helped Sarah to her feet. Their goodnights said, it wasn't until they were in her bedroom that the matriarch of the family spoke again.

'You didn't really want to go to the museum with Elliott, did you, Jade?'

Without waiting to think Jade opened her eyes wide and uttered a heartfelt, 'Heaven forbid!' before staring at Sarah in dismay. Perhaps she shouldn't have been quite so vehement in her opinion of one of the McGraths' guests. 'I'm sorry, Sarah . . .' she started to apologise, but her words were cut short by the older woman patting her knowledgeably on the arm.

'Don't be, don't be,' Sarah insisted. 'He wouldn't be my idea of a perfect escort either,' she chuckled.

Jade's relief was plain to see and she gave a low laugh. 'I'm so glad. I thought I might have committed a hideous *faux pas* there for a moment.' She glanced at the other woman suspiciously from the corner of her eye. 'You didn't happen to overhear what he was saying to me in the drawing room as well, did you?'

Sarah nodded her head unconcernedly, not in the least upset by the fact that some might have called it eavesdropping.

'Of course I did. It's my duty to have a care for the welfare of the company employees,' her eyes twinkled disarmingly. 'I thought your idea of telephoning him very commendable.' She paused thoughtfully. 'But is your time off really as badly arranged as all that? Perhaps I should speak to Tory about it.'

'Oh, no, Sarah, not you too! I wasn't complaining,' Jade hastened to assure her. 'It suits me fine the way it is and I don't really need any more time to myself—I have plenty for all I want to do.'

'But as Elliott so correctly said—it isn't right. You should have a whole day to yourself so that you could get completely away from the property if you want to. I'm afraid I've been very selfish—I've enjoyed your company so much that I've wholly restricted your movements.'

'Please, Sarah, don't say anything to Tory.'

A moment of intense scrutiny followed and then a relaxing, 'All right . . . if you don't wish me to. But you will have a full day off. Not tomorrow because Reid and Melissa will be arriving, but the day after. Yes, that's it,' Sarah congratulated herself. 'You can have Friday completely to yourself.'

Knowing that argument was useless once Sarah had really made up her mind, Jade accepted the decision ruefully. Whether she wanted to or not, she would not be working on Friday! Sarah had decreed it!

Another pause and, 'I'll have to let Tory know you won't be working, of course. Don't worry,' Sarah urged on catching sight of the apprehensive look on Jade's face, 'I'll tell him I've sent you to West Springs to do some shopping for me if you'd prefer it, although I really can't see why you're so averse to my speaking to him about it. I can assure you

Tory would be the first to agree that it's something you're fully entitled to.'

'Maybe so, but you know what Tory already thinks of me. Let's just say I don't want to take the chance of adding more fuel to the fire.'

'Rubbish, child! Why should it?'

'Sarah, *please*!'

'All right, if that's what you want,' a resigned Sarah agreed. 'Now just help me off with these pearls—my hands seem able to clasp them together easily enough, but it's a different matter entirely when it comes to taking them off— then you can either rejoin the party downstairs, or go along to your room. Whichever you'd rather.'

Having helped Sarah as much as she could—or was allowed—Jade returned to the gallery and stood looking down into the entrance below. She could hear the muted voices floating up from the drawing room and for a moment she was sure she heard Tory laugh. A tight band encircled her ribs at the sound, but with a vigorous denial to her pulsating emotions she resolutely turned towards her own room.

It was well over two hours later before Jade heard the first sounds of the departing guests moving out to their respective vehicles. A time during which sleep hadn't come and she had lain frustratedly staring into the darkness and listening to the constant chirping and whirring from the cicadas in the grounds below. The first of the cars began to move away and she found herself wondering whether Laura would go as she had come—with her brother—or whether Tory would be seeing her home. The idea that he might sent a lancing pain deep into Jade's heart and in a state very near to tears she rolled on to her side once more, closing her eyes tightly, and determinedly concentrated on waiting for the arms of Morpheus to come and claim her.

CHAPTER SEVEN

As predicted, Reid and Melissa McGrath, together with their two young children, arrived by plane the next morning. Reid, at thirty-two, was a tall brown-haired and blue-eyed version of his grandmother and had also inherited the innate McGrath charm in abundance. He obviously adored his petite, blonde, effervescent wife and was the very proud father of a six-year-old irrepressible bundle of energy called Derek, and an equally lovable little wistful-eyed four-year-old girl named Angela who dimpled delightfully whenever she smiled.

No sooner had the children tumbled out of the station wagon that had conveyed their family and luggage from the airstrip to the homestead than they had gone chasing down the hallway towards the library searching for 'Grandma'. That Sarah was actually their great-grandmother didn't worry them in the slightest. Nor did it worry Sarah, noted Jade with a smile, as she witnessed the wholehearted joy the children exhibited at being reunited with their oldest relative. The sound of more greetings flowed into the room from the hall.

'Tory, darling! Still as handsome as ever and still clinging tenaciously to your bachelor ways. It's good to see you again.'

'You too, Lissa,' came Tory's laughing return. 'And you're still as impudent as ever. Haven't you any respect for your elders? You should take a leaf from your daughter's book—now there's a child who really knows how to behave.'

'Don't say that, old son,' another laughing voice—Reid's—put in. 'As she grows older we're beginning to have our suspicions that Angela might have been a bit of a misnomer. Of late we've been thinking along the lines of Diavola—or whatever the feminine equivalent of the devil is. Our delightful little Angela isn't the angel she used to be.'

'Not to be wondered at—taking after her mother, I suppose.'

'Oh, unfair, Tory, unfair!' Lissa's melodious laugh sprang forth. 'How about the McGraths taking some credit? After all, I didn't produce her totally unaided.'

'Just so long as you look at Reid when you say that, Lissa, and not at me,' suggested Tory so drily that all three of them began laughing again.

Angela's small hand tugging at her mother's slacks and accompanied by an imperious, 'Mummy! Mummy! Come and see Grandma,' brought the mirth to a halt and the three adults followed their tiny guide back into the library.

Immediately their happy respects had been paid, and Jade introduced, Reid stage-whispered to his brother with a grin,

'Man, if that's the type of companion/secretary you're getting out here these days, a bushfire wouldn't stop me from coming home. How do you do it?'

A smile at his outrageous compliment touched Jade's lips, but Reid hadn't finished yet as, after a gleeful denial of Lissa's laughing protest he went on mock-seriously, 'But you really shouldn't knock her around like that, Tory. It's not the done thing, old son. He won't keep you that way, will he, Jade?' he inquired with a wink.

Jade didn't know quite how to answer and ended up by murmuring defensively, 'It's only for three months anyway, isn't it, Tory?'

'So the contract says.'

Carefully laconic and non-committal, she noted with some asperity. Although what she would have wanted him to say she couldn't have stated with any degree of certainty.

'All jokes aside, that is a nasty-looking bruise coming out on your cheek, Jade,' said Lissa sympathetically. 'You didn't by any chance collide with that swinging kitchen door, did you?'

Jade laughed. 'No, I ...'

'Fell off the crossing and tried a spot of body-surfing down the rapids.' Tory interjected, and continued for her: 'Only Jade was more fortunate than her ancestor ... she survived with just cuts and bruises.'

'Ancestor? More fortunate...?' Reid's face was a study of puzzled intentness until, 'Of course—*Pascoe*! Red Pascoe! Why ever didn't I tumble before? Especially with that red hair of yours,' he smiled at her. 'Did you know that Red had worked here before you came to the district, or has it all been an incredible coincidence?'

'Yes, I knew Red worked here, but we never guessed that we would—that is, my friend Helen and I—she's working with Jenny in the kitchen—be employed here too,' Jade explained. 'We had originally planned just to look over the area and then move on, but ...' She spread her hands wide expressively and left the outcome unsaid.

'Well, fancy that!' Reid clearly couldn't rid himself of amazement at such a turn of events, and Lissa's shivered, 'Fancy going down those rapids! One thing's for sure, *I* wouldn't have survived—I would have panicked!' had them all with sober thoughts in their minds.

'I might not have survived either,' admitted Jade slowly, 'if Tory hadn't come in after me.'

'Just as well he did then,' reflected Lissa, and gave her brother-in-law a teasing grin, 'but I can imagine he had a few choice words to say to you after he'd dragged you out again. Tory's not usually backward in letting you know what he's thinking, are you, Tory?'

'Can't afford to be with someone as shameless as you,' he retorted with an answering smile.

He isn't with me either, cried Jade inwardly. He makes it

139

all too plain what he thinks, but he's wrong all the same. Wrong, wrong, *wrong* . . .

By this time the children were becoming restless, so Sarah came up with a suggestion which gained their full and immediate approval.

'Why don't you go along and see Jenny in the kitchen? I'm sure she'll be able to find you a mug of milk each and something nice to eat,' she offered to them.

Derek was on his feet in a flash with a rushed, 'Thank you, Grandma,' and then he was through the doorway with Angela chasing after him as fast as her shorter legs would allow.

And that set the pattern for the remainder of the day— Derek and Angela having the time of their young lives as they rediscovered favourite people and haunts from previous visits—while Lissa and Reid held the attention of the older members of the household with the amusing and interesting tales they had brought with them.

Immediately after breakfast the next morning Sarah instructed Jane: 'Drive over to West Springs and have a nice relaxing day. We'll see you for dinner this evening. Lissa will look after me.'

But Jade didn't feel like driving to West Springs on such a hot day, for already the sun was a glaring ball in the eastern sky with not a hint of a cloud in sight, and there was nothing of great urgency that she needed to buy. Instead she meandered up the stairs and after wandering around her room disconsolately a few times hunched her shoulders decisively and made for the bottom drawer of the dressing table. She would go swimming. It was the perfect occupation in such weather and she had been told some days ago that the younger station hands often had a lot of fun in the water-hole some half mile or so above the causeway.

Dressed in a pretty lemon and green bikini, Jade pulled on a pair of faded denim shorts and a slim-fitting ribbed top. With a gaily patterned beach towel slung over one shoulder she skipped down the stairs and started along the passageway to the kitchen, intending to ask Jenny to let her make herself a packed lunch so that she could please Sarah by not returning to the house until late in the afternoon.

However, she had only just reached the swinging door when she heard voices coming from the front verandah. As she glanced round to see who was there her curious gaze turned to one of dismay. She could clearly see Laura mounting the front steps with Tory close at hand, but—horror of horrors—it was Elliott bringing up the rear that had caused the look of consternation. The thought of his persistent advances came shuddering to the front of her mind, and discarding her idea of seeing Jenny she hurtled down the rest of the passageway and out into the open air.

She hoped that she had managed to escape without being seen but, just to be on the safe side, she sprinted across the still damp lawn and into the cover of the shrubs and trees on the far side, where she stopped against the steel gateway to recover her breath. After a moment or two when her heart had stopped pounding from the unaccustomed hard exercise, she began to laugh quietly. That had been a near miss!

An unexpected, 'You know what they say? It's the first sign of madness . . . laughing to yourself,' had Jade whirling round nervously, but she collapsed on to the gate again in happy relief when she saw that it was only Gary.

'Oh, you gave me a fright,' she smiled up at him. 'I've just dodged out of Elliott Emery's way and I thought he'd found my hiding place!' She glanced over one shoulder back to the house. 'He hasn't come out this way, so perhaps I was lucky and he didn't see me.'

Gary pushed his hat to the back of his head, eyes dancing understandingly.

'I don't blame you for hiding from Elliott, but even so,

141

you can't stay here all day, Jade,' he pointed out with indisputable logic. 'Won't Sarah or Tory be looking for you?'

Jade shook her head. 'I'm free for the whole day. That's what worries me. If Elliott should find out I'm likely to be well and truly sunk!'

'In that case, we'll have to do something about it, won't we?' he came to her aid. 'As it happens, it's my day off too—I exchanged Sunday with Mike—and I was about to head up river to do a spot of fishing and swimming. Want to come along?' he invited cheerfully.

Jade couldn't believe her good fortune. 'Do I? Yes, *please!*' Another glance at the house and, 'Oh, God, there he is now—and he's coming this way,' her voice rose in panic. 'Can we leave at once, Gary? Do please say yes,' she begged.

'No sooner said than done, beautiful,' he agreed placidly. 'C'mon, this way,' he said, and placing a hand under each of her arms he swung her quickly over the fence and then, hand in hand, they were running for the protection of the machinery shed. Here they had to stop for a moment because they were both laughing too hard to continue. Jade leant back against the corrugated iron for support.

'It's just like the movies, isn't it?' she gasped. 'The goodies dodging around buildings and what-have-you in order to escape the baddie. I just wish I could pluck up enough courage to tell him to blast off, but as he's apparently a welcome guest I have the feeling it wouldn't go down very well if I did.'

Gary nodded sagely. 'You could be right,' he concurred. 'But we'd better be getting on, otherwise these goodies might yet be caught by the baddie.' He took hold of Jade's hand again and began tugging her along with him. 'The bike's just up here.'

A glance about her showed Jade the unevenness of the ground. 'Push-bike?' she marvelled, wide-eyed.

'No, you nut,' retorted Gary with a laugh, rumpling her

hair affectionately. 'Motor-bike. They're taking the place of horses in a lot of station work these days. There's less work and upkeep involved and they're a lot easier to transport. We've still got horses, of course—for some types of work they're invaluable—but more and more work's being done on bikes. Ever been on one before?' he smiled down at her.

'N-o,' she answered somewhat apprehensively.

'Don't worry, there's nothing to it. Just sit tight, hang on to me and we'll be there in no time at all.'

And there wasn't anything to it, Jade discovered happily. It was exhilarating speeding over the ground with a fresh breeze blowing in her face and her hair streaming out over her shoulders. Tucked up close behind Gary, gripping the seat with her knees and her hands resting loosely round his waist, she thrilled to the feel of unleashed power beneath her and the lean of the machine as they bypassed trees and boulders in their path. It was a fantastic way to see the countryside, too. All too soon the ride was over as Gary swung down an incline and brought the bike to rest among a clump of she-oaks standing beside the river's edge.

It was an idyllic day—the sun was hot and cheering while the water was cool and reviving. They fished and then swam and cooked Gary's catch in the small battered old frying pan he had packed in the pannier of the bike, and boiled up a billy of refreshing black tea with gum leaves added for that special distinctive flavour. The fish fell apart at a touch and went down sublimely, especially when accompanied by thick crusty slices of Jenny's fresh buttered bread. Dousing the fire with the last of their tea, they lay back contently in the shade watching the myriad shapes and forms produced by the sun filtering down through the dusty leaves. Jade smiled to herself. Sarah should be pleased—she was relaxing, and Marandoo, with all it entailed, was many miles from her thoughts.

Later in the afternoon they swam again, then gave themselves time enough to dry their swimsuits in the still warm air before donning their outer clothes, collecting the utensils they had used for their meal and checking that there was no risk of their fire bursting into renewed life the moment a slight breeze might blow up.

A short detour over less used, but more picturesque, trails filled in the remainder of their day and after a hair-raising ride down the side of the last rolling hill Gary eventually brought the bike sliding to a halt beside the machine shed. Lightly Jade swung off the machine and waited while he kicked the support into position.

'Thanks for a great day, Gary,' she smiled up at him. 'I really enjoyed myself.'

Gary grinned and placed a brotherly kiss on her forehead. 'The pleasure was all mine, beautiful. We'll have to see if we can't repeat it some other day. You're good company, Jade.'

'*Jade!*'

The last of Gary's words was repeated in a tone of suppressed violence and to her dismay Jade saw Tory striding purposefully towards the fence.

'Here we go again!' her eyebrows tilted philosophically and her mouth turned wry. 'I wonder what I'm supposed to have done now. I would have thought my absence for a whole day would have precluded my making any more mistakes.'

'Do you make that many?' inquired Gary.

'You'd be surprised! As far as Tory's concerned I can't do anything right!'

'Now, that *does* surprise me. I've always found Tory extremely easy to work for.'

'Jade!'

The voice was only one or two degrees less aggressive, and pushing her hair nervously back behind her ears Jade bade a hasty goodbye to Gary and with her towel flapping from her shoulder reluctantly went to meet Tory at the gateway. With a barely controlled impatience he held the gate open and snapped it shut savagely once she had passed through. She didn't have to wait long for the axe to fall.

'Don't you think Gary might be a little below the high standards you've set yourself for a husband?' he turned on her contemptuously. 'Apart from the fact that he happens to have a very nice girl down in the Riverina whom he's planning to become engaged to at the end of the year,' he added, with his eyes betraying a malicious satisfaction.

'Yes, I did know as a matter of fact,' Jade smiled, demurely sarcastic. 'Her name's Janice. Gary's told me all about her.'

'But that means nothing to you, of course. Does it amuse you to see if you can break up a well-balanced relationship between two nice people?'

Jade came back quickly. 'Don't be ridiculous, Tory. I'm not trying to break up anything. I can assure you I'm not interested in Gary as a prospective husband.'

'No?' Black brows rose disbelievingly. 'I didn't exactly see you trying to prevent him from kissing you just now!'

'Why should I? I like Gary, and it was only on the forehead after all. If it bothers you so much, just let's say I was collecting a memento of my stay at Marandoo.'

'In that case, let's see if we can't give you a souvenir you'll really remember, shall we?' he ground out explosively.

Suddenly his hand sank deep into her curling hair and she was pulled into his embrace with an overpowering force and held there by a rock-hard arm clamped around her back. Slowly and deliberately he pulled her head back and, much as she tried to evade that dangerously descending mouth, there was to be no escape, for his lips parted hers in a kiss that electrified her senses with a deadly proficiency and a hungry dominance that made her weaken treacherously.

145

When she thought she could stand the exquisite torment no longer his lips moved across her face to her warm arching throat where they continued to demolish her last defences with a consummate ease. An aching sob rose but was summarily stifled by the return of his passionate mouth so that she finally yielded to the demanding pressure and allowed the fire within to dictate her own uninhibited response.

All too soon Tory set her free and Jade swayed before him dazedly, her lips trembling as her eyes tried to pierce the shadows of the great overhanging branches of a riotously flowering poinciana in an attempt to read his expression.

'You're quite a girl, aren't you, honey?' he lashed her frayed emotions scornfully. 'But you're way off course if you think that tempting response of yours is going to make me change my mind about you. You forget ... I know exactly what your mercenary little plans are!' he continued in the same biting tones.

Did he think...? He couldn't think ... That she was making a play for himself? But that was what his words seemed to indicate. Oh, God, would he never stop making her pay for one chance remark? Her face tight from the rigid control she was exercising, Jade retorted with equal scorn.

'And to my way of thinking you're quite a guy too, Tory McGrath! Just remember that it was you who started the kissing, not me!' she had to remind him. 'If you feel you must exert your masculinity, why not try it on your girl-friend—I'm sure she would be only too pleased to accommodate you!' Hastily she stepped back as he moved menacingly closer. 'In the meantime, I wish you'd just leave me alone, because if you're an example of our wealthy society I wouldn't have one of you as a gift!' she hurled at him disparagingly before turning on her heel and running for the house as speedily as her shaking legs would carry her.

Tumbling into the dimly lit hall Jade slowed her pace a little and wheeled around the newel post, but there she halted, arrested by the figure of Laura immediately in front of her. The older girl's cold eyes raked Jade's dishevelled appearance spitefully.

'Oh, it's you,' she exclaimed. 'I've been hearing a lot about you—and your ancestor—today.' She didn't sound as if she had enjoyed the revelations. 'Is that why you came to Marandoo? To exact the family vengeance?' Laura tittered with an unconvincing show of humour.

'No.'

Jade's reply was short and explicit as she made to move past Laura, but the other girl shifted across the stair to block her passage once again.

'Has Sarah also told you about the rhyme?' she now asked, but with such a bland expression that Jade immediately became suspicious. 'Of course it's only two lines, but I've always thought they managed to convey the whole story so well.' She smiled lightly, but it didn't quite reach her eyes. 'Would you like to hear it?'

Interested in spite of herself, Jade nodded dumbly, wondering why Laura should have become so expansive all of a sudden. She wasn't kept in suspense for long.

' "Pascoe reached too high to ride,
    So Pascoe's Reach is where he died," '

quoted Laura with undisguised malice. 'Did you know that that is what they call the part of the river where they discovered his body—Pascoe's Reach?' she inquired all too informatively, and without waiting for an answer went on with silky insinuation, 'I do hope history doesn't repeat itself while you're here, Jade. It would be such a shame, and I'm sure my family wouldn't be able to come up with another rhyme to do full justice to the occasion—not as they did before.'

147

Two thoughts sprang immediately to Jade's reeling mind. First, that she should have known it would have been an Emery who penned those callous lines and, second, that Laura was for some reason warning her off! After her contretemps with Tory such a short while ago that idea seemed almost ludicrous, but ... who was she to deny Laura the pleasure of believing that a warning was necessary?

'It's very kind of you to be so concerned about my welfare, Laura, but there's no need to be. You see,' she smiled a slow secretive smile that conveyed a wealth of innuendoes, 'this Pascoe never reaches for anything she knows she can't obtain. It's a pity others don't always practise the same doctrine, don't you think?' she queried with brows innocently raised.

This time Jade succeeded in bypassing the girl before Laura could recover her thin veneer of composure as her face exploded into a vision of scarlet cheeks and venomously blue eyes, but the hissed, 'I'll get you for that, you little bitch ... just wait and see!' still managed to reach her at the head of the stairs.

A faint, remorseful smile pulled at Jade's mouth. It was funny how those that liked to dish the dirt never liked having any thrown back at them. They seemed to believe it was their sole prerogative. Normally she wasn't a catty person, but there was something about Laura's snide and contemptuous remarks that rubbed her the wrong way.

At least she should have been thankful to Laura for one thing, mused Jade a short time later while standing under the pelting streams of her invigorating shower, and that was for having dispelled those disquieting thoughts of Tory from her mind, if only for a little while, for now they were coming flooding back and she turned the tap off fretfully. But even a vigorous towelling of her wet hair couldn't keep them at bay for very long and with a resigned sigh she

148

made herself face the truth that she had been avoiding for so long.

She was in love with Tory McGrath! There was no skirting it—there was no disputing it—she had stupidly fallen in love with a man who had never failed to make it abundantly clear just what he thought of her! A man whose life-style was so completely removed from her own that, had she not brought herself so inauspiciously to his notice, he probably wouldn't even have deigned to bestow on her more than a fleeting glance. No wonder his kisses affected her so drastically, or that she could not—no matter how hard she tried—subdue her response to those kisses! What a laugh . . . Tory had said she'd come looking for a wealthy husband and she had to fall for one of the wealthiest of them all! Only she couldn't laugh, because she felt too close to tears!

Except for the return of Barbara with Nigel, her fiancé-to-be, the next week slipped by quietly. Quietly, that was, if you didn't consider the steady influx of relatives and acquaintances to the house and district and the extra work that seemed to be mounting daily.

On the following weekend the township of Wayamba held their annual picnic races which everyone from the surrounding area, and even those further afield, attended. It was a bright and sunny day and all the visitors at the homestead, together with most of the staff, had travelled out by mid-morning to the makeshift racecourse on the outskirts of the tiny township.

Tents had been set up to sell food and refreshments of all kinds, and long trestle tables with rustic type bench seats had been erected beneath the trees for those who wished to bring their own repasts. There were stalls selling snacks and treats for the children and pony rides to keep them amused while their parents discussed the merits and performances

149

of the listed runners. The track itself was outlined by a newly built split-log railing fence, and a saddling enclosure had been set aside for the horses and their riders.

By the time the McGrath party arrived the first race was due to begin and already there was a strong aura of the fairground about the scene. Where all the people had come from Jade and Helen—at last managing some moments together—couldn't imagine, but there were brightly dressed crowds wherever they looked. The children headed straight for the ponies, each armed with a stick of candy-floss for themselves and an apple for their chosen animal. Managing to find themselves a few spare inches along the rails, the girls were quickly joined by Gary and Mike.

'And what does your feminine intuition predict will win this event?' Gary's smile encompassed the two of them.

'We've had a little wager each on number three, Mandarin. Not that we know anything about any of them,' Jade explained with a grin, 'but we've decided we're only going to bet on black horses.'

Gary and Mike exchanged smiles across the heads of the two girls in between them.

'At times I guess that's as good a way as any to pick them,' confessed Mike with a reminiscent grimace. 'But what happens when there's two blacks in the same race?'

Now it was Jade and Helen's turn to look at each other—they hadn't considered that aspect.

'Toss a coin?' suggested Helen with a hopeful shrug.

'And if they're all black horses?' Gary was being happily difficult.

'Ah, in that case, we can't lose,' Jade laughed back at him.

'Okay, you win,' Mike admitted defeat in the face of that piece of indisputable reasoning. 'Just let's hope you're wrong this time—Gary and I have both gone for number one. There's not much of him, but we're hoping his early speed will do the trick for us.'

Jade scanned her programme quickly. 'Little Lucifer. Hmm, I like the name, but I'm sorry, fellas, you've made the wrong choice. I rather think he'll be a sick horse by the time the race is over.'

'What d'you mean ... sick?'

'What d'you know that we don't?' came two rapid questions.

'Only that he's bound to get pneumonia from the rush of air when Mandarin passes him, of course ... what else?' she laughed at their stricken faces.

Two sighs of relief, together with mock threats, greeted this statement, and then the announcer was calling the run of the race and all four of them were hanging over the rail and cheering their chosen favourites onwards. But, as Mike and Gary had foretold, Little Lucifer's early break on the field made the race for him and Mandarin hadn't been able to run him down, only coming to within a length of him as they reached the winning post.

'Bad luck, girls,' Gary consoled them, not quite concealing his own jubilant grin. 'But at least he came second— you did take him each way?'

Two dolefully shaking heads gave him his answer.

'But we will next time,' decided Helen with a rueful look.

And so the morning continued. The third race was for lady riders only and Jade was embarrassed to find herself shouting so vociferously for Ann Mason as the horses came pounding up the track, not just because she liked Ann, or that she happened to be riding a black horse—in this particular race Jade would have been quite willing to change her system—but because she beat an immaculately turned out Laura Emery by a good five lengths.

After that Jade and Helen made their way back to the tables which they began covering with pretty patterned cloths, ready for the prepared dishes of food from the great hampers that had been brought with them. By the time the fourth race was concluded everything was laid out on the tables and the announcer called a halt in the proceedings in order that everyone could replenish themselves for the afternoon's entertainment.

Before the crowd became too thick around the tables Jade filled two plates with a variety of food, collected two pairs of knives and forks as well as a few paper napkins and took them over to where Sarah was comfortably seated in her own chair in the shade of the great spreading branches of a Moreton Bay fig tree. Carefully handing over one of the plates to Sarah, Jade swiftly spread out a rug on the ground beside the chair and sat down.

Sarah tasted a forkful of orange and cheese flan and smiled.

'Hmm, very nice—one of Jenny's best.' She looked down at the bright head beside her. 'And how does young Helen like working in our kitchen, Jade?'

A smiling face tipped upwards. 'She loves it. Says she's learning a whole host of hints and tips that she never even guessed at before.'

A short pause and then a wry, 'Mike Johnson should be pleased,' from Sarah.

Jade rapidly swallowed her mouthful of ham and pineapple. Although Sarah didn't get about much, there wasn't a lot that went on that she didn't know.

'Yes, I have the feeling that those two are quite serious about one another,' she admitted with a thoughtful smile, then, 'although nothing definite has been settled yet, as far as I know,' in case she had confessed to something that Helen would rather have had kept secret.

'What will you do if they do decide they want to get married?'

'I haven't really thought all that much about it,' she shrugged. 'Continue on my own, I guess. It would seem a bit of an anticlimax if I went back to Melbourne right now.'

Sarah took her time and thoughtfully chewed through

152

another piece of flan. 'You would be welcome to stay on here ... that is, if you can put up with a querulous old woman like me.'

'You're not querulous,' denied Jade emphatically, amazed that Sarah should even think herself so. 'As for putting up with you,' she laughed softly, 'you make me feel a fraud for accepting wages as your companion most of the time. It's always—"take a couple of hours off, Jade," or, "Go and see if your friend has some free time to spend with you." Why, even this morning it was, "You go and see the races, Jade, you've not seen them before. I can manage on my own." I've never worked for anyone easier than you.'

'Then you'll consider staying?' Sarah sounded pleased.

Would she? Jade sighed. She'd love it ... and hate it. So near to Tory ... and yet so far. Somehow she didn't think she could stand it; even this last week had proved an almost unbearable strain in controlling her thoughts and actions. But Sarah was waiting for an answer.

'I will consider it,' she replied quietly, but she had no doubt what her eventual answer would have to be.

'Champagne, Sarah ... Jade?'

Suddenly the object of Jade's thoughts took on a very real presence as Tory stood on the other side of Sarah's chair, a pearled bottle of wine in one hand with wisps of vapour still circling from its open neck, and two frail-looking glasses in the other. Dressed in dark brown pants with a peppermint green short-sleeved knitted shirt and with an utterly charming smile as he looked at Sarah, he was, Jade felt, the most striking personification of the dangerously exciting and powerful male she had ever seen.

'Lovely,' commented Sarah with satisfaction after taking a sip from the glass Tory handed her. 'Of course Jade will have some,' she nodded to her grandson commandingly, 'it's just what we need with our salad.'

On the point of refusing, Jade now acquiesced resignedly with downcast eyes and a low murmured, 'Thank you,' as

153

she accepted the sparkling drink from his outstretched hand.

For a few moments Tory sank down on to his haunches beside Sarah, but while they were talking Jade studiously kept her head averted and made a great show of looking over the crowds between the many tents and stalls and the various modes of dress. Little did she know that for some time after his departure Sarah had been inspecting her pensive profile intently. Her first indication came as something of a shock.

'Well? What are you going to do about it?' was the sudden demand.

A frown creased her forehead as Jade swung around. 'I—I'm sorry—I think I must have missed something.' Her head tilted sideways. 'Do about what?' she inquired.

'About putting a smile back on that pretty face of yours, that's what!' was the bald retort. 'I told you I didn't like sour faces around me.' A tiny hand pointed to Jade's cheek. 'You may have recovered from your lacerations, but you've replaced them with the beginnings of dark circles under your eyes, and I like those even less.'

A sip from her glass gave Jade time to come up with a near-excuse.

'I'm sorry, Sarah, I—er—I haven't been sleeping too well this past week. I—um—suppose that must be the reason,' she finished lamely.

'You think so?' drily.

'What else could it be?' she asked with wide innocent eyes, hoping against hope that the matter would be pushed no further.

Sarah's brows rose fractionally. 'You would know better than I,' she averred slowly, her gaze penetrating. 'Although that still doesn't explain the drooping mouth, does it?'

'No—well, I expect I've just had a fit of the blues,' Jade made herself laugh lightly, and scrambling to her feet she brushed the seat of her pants nervously and changed the subject. 'Would you like something for dessert? There's fruit salad, or trifle, or fresh fruit if you would prefer.'

Cornflower blue eyes held wary green ones for what seemed a lifetime to the younger girl before Sarah sighed softly.

'All right, Jade. I will have some fruit salad and cream, thank you.'

With an almost visible relaxing of taut muscles, Jade moved around Sarah's chair, but then a hand on her wrist halted her once more.

'Just remember, Jade ... if you want something you have to go after it. Very little is ever achieved without some sort of personal effort.'

She averted her head from that sympathetic glance swiftly. 'I will remember, Sarah ... thank you,' she whispered, and hurried on, her thoughts in turmoil.

Just what had Sarah meant by those words? Jade could not bring herself to accept the easy solution that Sarah had guessed how she felt about Tory. No, it had to be something else, surely. Ideas raced disjointedly through her mind. Suddenly one stayed longer than the rest. Ah, could that perhaps be it? Sarah knew she had been seeing Gary—she also knew that she had spent her free day with him last week. She must have concluded that Jade's introspection this last week had been caused by Gary's not reciprocating her affections. That would *have* to be it! Already she began to feel a little better. Poor Gary, she smiled ruefully to herself, but at least it was better than Sarah guessing the truth—*anything* would be better than that!

'Why so thoughtful, Jade? Can't you decide on your next winner?' Lissa's laughing voice broke into her thoughts.

A quick shake of her head sent the disturbing ideas from her mind and she smiled in return.

'No—I was just wondering whether to join Sarah in having a dessert.' She was surprised how easily the lie came to her lips.

155

'In that case, wonder no more—have the trifle. It's superb.'

'That good?'

'Absolutely. Ask Angela. She has the ferreting out of the choicest dessert down to a fine art,' Lissa confirmed indulgently.

As from nowhere the specialist now appeared on the scene, her sticky face and fingers infallible evidence of the enjoyment to be gained from a bowl of trifle.

'Can me have some more, Mummy?' she wheedled unashamedly.

'Can *I* have some more, darling,' Lissa corrected her gently.

A puzzled frown settled on Angela's childish forehead. 'Not you, Mummy,' she informed her mother solemnly. '*Me*!'

Jade and Lissa swiftly suppressed their laughter. 'I give up,' Lissa smiled. 'I'll try again next year—when she's a little older.' And to her daughter. 'Yes, darling, you can have some more—but only a little. We don't want to upset that cast-iron stomach of yours.'

'What's cars-ion, Mummy?'

'Something that's very strong and can take a lot of punishment without showing any signs of wear. Amazingly similar to what your tummy always appears to be, my pet,' said Lissa, taking Angela's hand in her own and leading her back to the now less laden table with Jade by their side.

'Hi there, where did you disappear to?' Gary ranged up beside Jade as she began ladling fruit salad and cream into a bowl for Sarah and trifle for herself.

She nodded towards the old fig tree. 'Over there with Sarah. You didn't think I was going to sit with you and the rest of the riff-raff, did you?' she teased cheekily.

'Watch it, kid,' he warned with a broad grin, grabbing her tightly round the waist, 'or you'll find yourself wearing that trifle instead of eating it!'

A laughing Lissa put a finger across her lips. 'Sssh!' she pleaded. 'Saying such a thing in Angela's presence is as good as seeing it done.'

'And wouldn't that make a nice ending for lunch,' commented Gary, taking one of the bowls from Jade and draping his other arm casually over her shoulders. 'Come on, I think we'd better beat a hasty retreat before young Angela does something drastic.'

When they had rejoined Sarah, Gary stretched long legs out before him as he leant back relaxedly against the trunk of the tree next to Jade.

'Ah, Gary. It's nice to see you. Have you been looking after my companion for me?' Sarah smiled, and it was plain to see that these two had a lot of time for each other.

'Doing my best, Sarah,' he told her. 'But she's a bit of a handful. I don't know how you put up with her.'

'I have my methods,' chuckled Sarah knowingly, her expression almost affectionate as she surveyed the laughing face of the young girl by her chair. 'Have you decided who's going to take out the Wayamba Cup this year, Gary, or are you going to be like me and stay loyal to the property?'

Gary fished a somewhat crumpled programme from the back pocket of his pants and proceeded to flick through the paper quickly until he came to the appropriate page.

'Like you, I'm staying faithful, Sarah,' he told her after scanning the short list of runners. 'I reckon Tory's Fluid Power will be the one to toss, but I have to admit that Harry Rickards has worked that roan of his into fine shape. It could go either way, I guess.'

'Has Tory entered a horse?' Jade now asked in surprise, suddenly searching her own programme with interest. 'Is he riding it?'

'No, young Eric Preston is,' Gary was the one to enlighten her before turning conspiratorially to Sarah. 'I ask you, what sort of a girl is that? Here we've been talking of nothing else all week, and she doesn't even know there's one entered!' He shook his head in mock despair.

'I'm afraid Jade has been away in a world of her own for the past week,' Sarah took it on herself to explain drily. 'Perhaps you can make an effort to bring her back to earth while you're with her today, Gary.'

Jade gave her a faintly suspicious glance. Was that her way of trying to help with what she assumed to be Jade's problems? Oh, well, even if it was it did no harm, and as she *did* enjoy Gary's company she might as well go along with it.

'I suppose you're going to be a traitor to the camp and not back the McGrath entrant,' Gary suggested slyly to Jade, a twinkle in his eye. 'Seeing that our horse is a chestnut and not a black.'

'Well, they do say it brings bad luck to change horses— hah, very appropriate—in midstream,' murmured Jade absently, riffling through the pages of her programme once more. 'Is there a black in the race?'

'With a good chance too,' he confirmed.

'Then perhaps I'd better ...' her words faded away when she saw who was listed as the owner of the black entrant— Elliott Emery—and she gave Gary a mock-threatening look. 'No, I've changed my mind,' she amended rapidly. 'I wouldn't want anyone to think I was being disloyal—I'll support Fluid Power,' she smiled triumphantly at him before turning to her employer. 'Will you be coming down to watch this one, Sarah?'

'No, child. I prefer to watch from the comfort of my own chair. From here I get a good view with the aid of these,' and Sarah patted a pair of powerful-looking binoculars tucked down the side of her seat which Jade hadn't noticed before.

'Well, I'd better get moving,' Jade now suggested, springing gracefully to her feet, 'otherwise Helen and I won't have finished all the clearing up before the race is due to start,' and she began by stacking their own plates and bowls into a neat pile.

'Yes, get cracking. You don't want to miss the most important event of the day.' This came from a contented Gary in a comfortable position with a freshly lit cigarette between his fingers.

Taking the opportunity, Jade turned to him with a smile. 'Is that an offer of help?' she inquired demurely.

He threw up his hands in surrender. 'Caught again! The things I do for you,' he laughed, rising to his feet and taking the pile of plates from her unresisting fingers. 'Go on then,' he adjured, in assumed resignation. 'You go and help Helen put them wherever they're supposed to go while I scout round and collect all the strays and leftovers.'

With Mike roped in to help as well the four of them made short work of clearing the tables, and it wasn't long before everything was packed awaiting their return to the homestead.

A hurried, 'I'll see you all down on the fence. I'd better check that Sarah's okay,' and Jade sped off in the direction of the fig tree, but having ascertained that Sarah had all she needed, she couldn't rediscover her former companions' whereabouts. Their gaily clad figures appeared to be missing from the crowd already lining the rails, so with an expressive shrug of her shoulders Jade made for a small space still vacant. No sooner had she squeezed herself in than a hand familiarly spanned her waist and warm breath fanned her ear.

'Come to cheer me in a winner, have you, sweetie?' Elliott's honeyed tones grated, while the offensive grasping of his warm hand sent shudders down Jade's spine and she tried to squirm away from his unpalatable proximity.

'Actually, I haven't,' she was pleased to be able to confess. 'I've come to cheer for Tory's horse.' She felt her temper rising as his hand became more venturesome. 'But, in the meantime, I'd be pleased if you would keep your hands to yourself!' she snapped through gritted teeth.

His eyes took on an icy expression at her rebuff of his advances, but his hand stayed where it was.

'Come off it, sweetie, we all know what goes on in the modelling world. Don't try making yourself out to be a little Miss Innocent with me—I know your sort too well.'

'In that case, perhaps you'd better do as you were asked, Elliott . . . and remove your hand,' a cold voice suggested in an inflexible tone, causing both of them to swing around and meet Tory's slate-coloured implacable gaze.

Jade blessed his intervention, pleading with green eyes made huge with apprehension for him to understand that the situation had come about through no encouragement on her part.

'What's it to you, Tory?' Elliott seemed to slur his words somewhat, making Jade wonder whether he had had too much to drink with his lunch. 'God knows, you're no saint when it comes to women. Or is it because you couldn't make the grade with this one, eh?' he insinuated craftily.

Her cheeks burning fiercely, Jade glanced round frantically at the surrounding crowd, dreading to think that others could overhear the conversation, but luckily there appeared to be enough noise going on around them to cover their voices and, as yet, their tones were low—Tory's dangerously so.

Now his mouth tightened with the control he placed upon himself, but his words cut like a whip.

'I think you've said enough, Elliott! In future I suggest that if you can't handle your drink, you shouldn't imbibe quite so freely! As my employee, Jade is my responsibility —do I make myself clear? Or would you like me to say more?' he questioned contemptuously.

For a moment Elliott attempted to outstare him, but in the end it was his eyes that fell and with something remarkably like a snarl he pushed Jade against Tory's side.

'Take her then, if you feel so strongly about it. She probably wouldn't be worth the trouble anyway!' he threw in a parting shot as he stormed his way through the crowd.

With her head downbent Jade concentrated unhappily on watching her fingers twine together and then free themselves again. Tory still hadn't spoken to her directly, but she knew he was still there because a length of long leg was clearly visible through her lashes. She swallowed nervously before changing a swift glance upwards.

At last she murmured disjointedly, 'I'm sorry, Tory ... I didn't ... I wasn't—encouraging him.' A shivering breath. 'Please—I want you to believe that.'

'I know you weren't,' he agreed softly, one hand absently smoothing over the long sweep of her hair behind her ear while his eyes never strayed from the curves of her slightly trembling lips. 'I'm sorry too that Elliott lost his control to such an extent that he considered his insinuations would be acceptable—to either of us.'

Jade only just managed to nod her head in recognition, so fascinated was she by the intense and delightfully gentle expression in those grey eyes which had her heart tumbling to her feet and back again before she could drag her own eyes away. The spell was broken and she cleared her throat uncomfortably.

'We'd better watch the race,' she laughed shakily. 'I—I— think they're under the starter's orders now,' and she whirled around to lean against the railing for support.

Muscular brown hands clasped the rail on either side of her, imprisoning her within the most exciting cage she could ever have imagined. She could feel the solidity of his chest hard against her back as they both leaned forward in order to obtain a better view, and knew her quivering emotions to be running wild. But there was nothing she could do to influence them into a more stable state, and after a moment or two she began to relax and permitted herself the enjoyment of relishing the stimulating nearness of the body of the man she was in love with.

161

Almost uninterestedly Jade saw a cluster of horses—sinews tautented, hooves flashing—as they thundered up the slight incline towards the finishing post, but the excited roar of the crowd finally penetrated her bemused brain and when she saw that it was a black horse in the lead her nails dug into the palms of her hands as she clenched her fists and willed that the flying chestnut on the outside would over take it. It did. In a flurry of speed it bounded past the fading black to win by an easy margin.

Amidst the enthusiastic cheering she spun round to Tory. 'He won!' she exclaimed as animatedly as if she owned the horse herself, her eyes glowing greenly. 'He really did! You've won the Cup!'

Tory's teeth showed startlingly white against the bronze of his skin. 'You sound as though you didn't expect he would,' he accused with a laugh. 'But just to prove that it really did happen,' he caught one of her hands lightly with his own, 'why don't you come with me to collect it?'

'I couldn't!' she gasped, dragging her hand from his regretfully and looking towards the judges' stand. 'But you'd better go. I think they're looking for you.'

'Congratulations, darling!' Laura swept on to the scene dressed in a beautiful sky blue silk blouse and pale cream jodhpurs of impeccable cut, to kiss Tory possessively on the mouth and tuck her arm confidingly in his. 'We nearly had you that time, but it doesn't seem to have been a day for the Emerys.' Her gaze moved round to encompass Jade in its chillingly malicious appraisal. 'Never mind, our turn will come, I'm sure,' she let icy fingers of apprehension trail down Jade's spine before smiling back at Tory. 'Shall we go and collect the Cup now, darling?'

It was that last nonchalant endearment signifying ownership that had Jade thrusting past them blindly with what she hoped was a gay and carefree, 'I must find the others,' before losing herself in the throng milling round the finishing post.

She couldn't have stood there a moment longer watching Laura devour Tory with her eyes, or to see him smile back at her in return. Especially not after those few glorious never-to-be-forgotten minutes when she and Tory had, for the first time, seemed so close and all antagonistic thoughts had been buried. Of only one thing was she sure—moments like that would never come her way again.

CHAPTER EIGHT

JADE did very little typing during the next week, for the following Saturday was the big day, but she was kept extremely busy all the same, as were the rest of the staff, in making sure that all was in readiness and that all the necessary preparations had been made.

There were telephone calls to and from various relatives advising times of arrival—mostly by private plane, it seemed—and calls to the caterers, musicians and photographers making sure that nothing had been forgotten. Barbara's dress for the occasion hadn't been ready when she had returned to the homestead the week before, so there were extra calls to a cousin in Brisbane reminding her that, whatever she did, she mustn't forget to bring it with her.

Except during the evenings the house seemed to be full of nothing but women that week, the men—as with one accord—having decided to make themselves scarce among such a gathering of enthusiastic females.

Saturday morning had been set aside for the women to attend the hairdressing salon in West Springs and, much to her surprise, Jade found that this invitation included herself too. In the end there were two car loads of females desirous of having their hair coiffured for the party that would make headlines in most of the country's major newspapers and magazines. Jade went with them, for a seed of an idea had begun to germinate in her brain. She still occasionally smarted with remembrance of Tory's 'that damned hair' and had decided that, once and for all, he would not be able to repeat his remark.

So, while the others were having their hair piled into elegant styles, Jade was having hers cut, and cut as short as was reasonably possible. By the time it had been washed and set, it framed her face in perky ruffled curls that drew attention to her wide-spaced eyes and exposed a tender length of jawline. That it suited her there was no doubt, but the exclamations of woe from Sarah, Lissa and Barbara over the loss of her beautiful long hair were numerous. On the way home she couldn't help putting an exploring hand to her head from time to time. It felt strange to have no hair resting on the nape of her neck and it made her seem oddly defenceless, but it was definitely a lot cooler. And that, she convinced herself, was the most important thing.

During the afternoon the caterers flew in with their myriad cartons and containers, and took over the kitchen. As Sarah was taking her usual rest and Helen had been made almost superfluous in the kitchen, the two girls made the most of their opportunity and headed for Jade's room for a little relaxation and a quiet chat before the strenuous evening ahead. Jade was swinging bare feet over the side of the bed while Helen was sitting cross-legged on the end of it, resting her back against the corner post.

'I've noticed you haven't mentioned Mike much this last week,' Jade probed gently, reaching for a packet of cigarettes and lighting one. 'Aren't things going as well as they might be in that direction?'

Helen bent to inspect the hem of her slacks which she had been pleating industriously.

'As a matter of fact,' she began slowly, hesitantly, 'he's asked me to marry him,' and her eyes flew to Jade's to gauge her reaction.

'Well, well, who would have guessed it?' teased her friend with a grin. 'And what did you say? ... as if I can't guess! Or can't I?' she laughed.

Making a grab for the cigarettes, Helen lit one of her own. 'You can,' she admitted drily. 'I guess it must have been pretty obvious. Even Sarah asked me the other day when I was going to marry the man and put him out of his misery. You know how candid Sarah can be,' she smiled.

Jade's eyes widened understandingly. 'And how!' she concurred. 'And just when *are* you going to marry the man?' she now asked.

Helen went back to pleating her slacks. 'Well, Mike wants it to be as soon as possible, but I said I'd have to see you first.'

'Why me? You don't need my permission.'

'Because we agreed to come on this trip together. I feel I'd be letting you down terribly if I opted out so early in the piece.'

'Don't be so silly! I may be your best friend, but even *I* don't expect to be rated higher than a husband,' Jade smiled. 'Go and get married ... I give you both my blessing and wish you well. Just don't forget to send me lots of photos when the babies start arriving.'

'Goodness, don't rush us!' protested a laughing Helen. 'I rather think I'd like to have him to myself for a while. At the moment I don't even want to share him with our children.' She looked at Jade questioningly. 'Is that too awful of me?'

Jade pondered the question seriously, drawing deeply on her cigarette. 'I don't think so,' she offered eventually. 'After all, you are supposed to be marrying because you love *him*. And there must be many adjustments to be made on both sides once you start living together, which I should imagine would be a lot easier to make if there's only the two of you. How's that?' she inquired. 'You now have the full benefit of my total spinsterly—or should it be bachelorette?—experience.' A short pause and then, 'I think the best advice I can give is for the two of you to play it by ear. How could I possibly advise anyone what to do in their marriage? I've never even been engaged—let alone married!'

Helen's laughter was soon replaced by a worried frown.

'But what will you do, Jade? Will you continue the trip on your own? Do you think it wise to?'

'Possibly not, but knowing me I more than probably will. There's a lot of places I'd still like to see and with no ties,' how that statement hurt these days, 'then I may as well keep going. Who knows? I may meet another girl in Brisbane or somewhere along the way with similar ideas to mine.'

'Not possible to find another girl with ideas quite like yours,' teased Helen, stretching her legs out in front of her and clasping her hands behind her head. 'Which reminds me—I never did get to ask you where did the idea come from for the haircut? I got the shock of my life when I saw you come back.'

'Oh, that,' Jade put a hand self-consciously to her newly short hair. 'It was too hot the other way and I decided on a change, that's all,' she excused herself offhandedly. 'Why? Don't you like it?'

'Very much,' nodded Helen vigorously. 'But it's so different it will take a while for me to get used to it. If I remember correctly it's been years since you had it that short.'

'Mmm, not since we were in school.'

The girls continued their desultory conversation for another half an hour or so before Helen checked the time with her watch and hurriedly took her departure. Jade showered at leisure and splashed on some refreshing cologne before slipping into lacy wisps of underwear and throwing open the door to her wardrobe.

Not that she had a choice to make—neither she nor Helen had expected to indulge in much night-life on their trip and there was only one dress that was really suitable—but it hadn't been cheap and the cut was perfect for her. By no means was it *haute couture* as the greater percentage of dresses worn by the women guests that night would be, but she didn't consider it would let her down too badly. In

167

sheer black chiffon that brought out the burning fire in her hair and the creamy texture of her skin, it was all curve and shape from the plunging halter neckline to the floating accordion-pleated skirt that swirled gently round her ankles.

When she was finally ready Jade took a last critical look at herself in the mirror. Warm golden skin, thick dark lashes surrounding glowing green eyes and inviting apricot-tinged lips all told her the same thing—she had never looked better in her life, and she expelled her breath thankfully. For some reason she felt she needed every morsel of confidence if she was to survive this particular evening without carrying everlasting scars.

Almost guiltily she stepped out into the corridor and closed her door quietly, turning towards Sarah's suite. Before she could reach the door, however, footsteps sounded taking the stairs two at a time and a lean and lithe Tory bounded into view.

Obviously he was heading for a shower because he was still dressed in working clothes, his dark hair curling on to his forehead, but as soon as he sighted Jade his step slowed and long-fingered hands were thrust into the back pockets of denim jeans as, with a long drawn-out, 'My God...!' he approached her slowly, his assessment thorough and inescapable.

Jade licked her lips nervously when he came to a halt before her, but even so she wasn't prepared for the low, infuriated, 'What the hell have you done to your hair?' that seemed to explode from him.

Again her hand strayed to her vulnerable nape and she found herself stammering defensively, 'I—I...' then swallowed and pulled herself together—after all, it was none of his business what she did with her hair. 'It used to get in the way and—and it was *annoying*,' she emphasised the last acidly.

A flicker of recognition traced its way over Tory's face and his eyes stabbed at her angrily.

'And that's supposed to be a reason?' he speculated incredulously.

'It was enough for me,' Jade was goaded on to the defensive again, her eyes falling before his.

'Well, it's not for *me*!' came the unequivocal retort, and she trembled to feel his hand rumpling through her short curls. 'I've never before in my life met anyone quite so perverse as you, honey. I can't make out whether you do it on purpose, or if it just comes naturally.' The exasperated satire stung, but before she could reply his hand had left her hair and forced her chin up so that she had no option but to meet his gaze. 'Let it grow again, Jade,' he suggested gently. 'I don't like it short.'

'You don't have to,' she rebuffed the appeal in his voice by telling herself that if she weakened now he could all too easily discover how she felt about him.

All was still immediately following her deliberately worded repudiation and it was with something like regret that she felt his hand leave her chin and heard him concede quite indifferently, 'No, I don't, do I?' before moving past her and entering his own bedroom.

Jade leant weakly against the wall, her heart pounding a suffocating rhythm, and tried to convince herself she had been right in so summarily dismissing the only proprietorial comment Tory had ever made to her. The trouble was, only one half of her agreed with this action, the other half was only too desirous of doing exactly as he wished.

Composing her slightly distraught features as much as possible, she entered Sarah's room slowly after her light knocking had been acknowledged and found her seated before her dressing table and looking her most imperial in powder-blue French silk jersey, her neck, wrist and ears adorned with the most eye-catching array of diamonds and sapphires that Jade had ever seen outside a shop, while her hair was swept regally high.

'Ah, Jade,' Sarah called directly she had closed the door.

169

'Come here, child, and help me with my make-up if you will. These sapphires drain every last vestige of colour from my face and I want to use some of this blusher,' she handed over a small tortoiseshell container, 'but I'm afraid my hand isn't steady enough for me to apply it nowadays and I don't want to look like a painted doll,' she explained whimsically.

Happy to have something to take her mind from less satisfactory thoughts, Jade withdrew the tiny brush from its resting place inside the small box and with light feathery strokes applied the becoming colour gently to Sarah's cheeks. Standing back to survey her work, she tilted her head consideringly.

'I don't think you need any more than that, do you?'

Sarah turned back to her mirror discerningly, looking at her reflection and nodding her head with satisfaction.

'No, that's just enough, thank you, Jade,' she smiled. 'Now if you'll just lend me your arm I can make it downstairs and see that everything is going smoothly before the first of our guests arrive.' She patted Jade's hand encouragingly as they moved to the door. 'You look very beautiful tonight, child. I can see I shall have to keep you close by my side or I shall find one of our young men wanting to whisk away my young companion for good,' she said humorously.

Jade accepted the compliment with a light laugh although it hurt unbearably to make the effort, but she couldn't allow Sarah to guess at her true feelings. As it was Jade could quite easily see herself being more than content to spend the whole of the evening by Sarah's side. In that way she might be able to avoid all but the barest contact with anyone present, and she didn't need to remind herself to whom that thought was chiefly directed.

Downstairs Jenny and Helen were putting the finishing touches to the delightful bowls and vases full of fresh flowers that bedecked the drawing room where the carpets had been removed to reveal a huge expanse of polished floorboards suitable for dancing, and all but a necessary minimum of furniture had been transferred elsewhere. The caterers were still supervising the arrangement of the tables in the dining room, while the quartet of some renown that had been flown in to provide the musical entertainment were busily tuning their instruments on the small raised dais at their disposal, and the photographers with their cameras and electronic flash equipment were hurrying here and there checking angles, apertures and degrees of light and shade.

Laughter sounded in the hallway and Barbara and Nigel entered the drawing room, closely followed by Lissa and Reid. The two girls looked stunning in pale lemon rough silk and turquoise shantung respectively while the men were resplendent in dark evening dress with snowy-white lace-ruffled shirts.

'How about a drink to ease the nerves?' suggested Reid brightly, his glance covering all present. 'I always did hate this hanging around until the first guests arrive.'

'Good idea,' agreed Nigel, running a finger around the inside of his shirt collar. 'I feel I could do with one.'

'Not getting cold feet, are you, my love?' chipped Barbara with a smile, slipping her arm about his waist.

Nigel caught her close with an arm about her shoulders. 'What? And miss out on all that lovely loot of yours?' he grinned down into her eyes.

As it was perfectly clear that Nigel was far from short of a dollar or two of his own, this remark brought forth spontaneous laughter from all of them, even Jade, although she couldn't help comparing the different attitude that resulted when Nigel passed such a comment to the storm she had aroused through making a casual utterance in the same vein. She heaved a sigh. One law for the rich—and one for the poor. There always had been and, she guessed, there always would be. It was an incontrovertible fact of life!

171

Reid's voice broke into her reverie, causing her to raise her head and see Tory standing in the doorway, head slightly bent as he put the dancing flame of a lighter to the end of his cigarette before coming into the room with a long-legged stride, a smile catching at the corners of his firm mouth.

'Tory! We're just about to adjourn to the dining room for a pre-party drink. At least I think that's where they've arranged for them to be served,' Reid smiled.

'Attempting to bolster Nigel's failing nerves, are we?'

'Pay no attention to him, Nigel,' Reid advised with a dire look in his brother's direction. 'He's only so sure of himself because he still has his freedom and we haven't, but you mark my words, he'll fall hard pretty shortly and *then* we'll see a difference.' He laughed with devilish humour at the thought.

Tory chuckled amiably. 'Not likely, young brother. Or haven't you heard ... that with age comes wisdom?' he retorted.

'No man was ever lucky enough to be *that* wise,' retaliated Reid, and earned himself a poke in the ribs from his wife.

'Watch it darling,' she warned him merrily. 'I'm keeping score.'

Reid pulled a grimace of assumed fear. 'In that case, we'd better go quickly to the bar so that I can fortify myself for the reckoning when it comes,' he suggested banteringly.

Before the rest of the house-guests had time to join them for more than one drink the first of the visitors began arriving, and after an hour had passed Jade began to wonder where the remainder that were still to come would fit in. The house already seemed full to overflowing with chattering, laughing people as they sauntered from room to room, mingling first with one group here, another there, and still more dancing to the lilting strains of the quartet.

A whispered, 'Have you seen the presents laid out in the

172

library?' had her spinning around to face Helen and shaking her head negatively. Helen's eyes opened wide expressively. 'You should! They must be worth a king's ransom!'

'Not surprising really, is it?' Jade whispered back out of the corner of her mouth. 'I mean to say, just look at some of the outfits here tonight. I'd hate to think what some of them cost.'

'Maybe, but you go and have a look at the presents all the same,' Helen gave her a gentle push towards the appropriate doorway. 'As they say in the classics—you ain't seen nothin' yet!'

Standing in the middle of the library a few minutes later Jade had to admit that her friend had been right. Up until now—she hadn't seen anything! Everywhere she looked there were beautiful gifts laid out on their beds of pretty wrapping paper or delicate tissue paper, each one more impressive than the last. Shining silver, sparkling crystal, translucent porcelain and twinkling chromium—they were all there, every type of gift imaginable.

'I hope it doesn't prove too great a temptation for you to go back into the family business.'

At the sound of Laura's disparaging voice Jade turned reluctantly to meet her cold blue gaze. Just inside the door, a glass of champagne in her hand and dressed in a flattering creation of flowing coral, Laura was at her most haughty.

'I'm sorry, I'm not sure I understand you,' Jade frowned, although she understood the tone well enough. 'The family business...?'

A mocking sneer marred Laura's features. 'Well, you must admit that your ancestor didn't come to this country voluntarily. He was a thief, wasn't he?'

The brazen suggestion—it couldn't possibly have been called an innuendo—took Jade's breath away.

'Are you implying that ... that I was intending to steal some of these things?' she gasped.

'Who knows?' Laura's shoulders lifted suggestively. 'I

173

may have arrived at an inopportune moment ... I may not.'
But her implication was plain.

'How dare you!' Two spots of colour burned high on
Jade's cheeks and her eyes blazed. 'My family may not be
as wealthy as yours, Miss Emery, but I am pleased to be
able to say that their moral character has improved over the
years. I wonder if you can say the same for yours,' she gave
her scorn full rein.

Laura's mouth twisted smugly—she was very sure of
herself.

'My family's morals aren't in question here—yours are!
We all know why you came here—your type's all the same,
out for whatever you can get your hands on!' she derided.
'Well, we don't want your kind at Marandoo and I, for one,
shall make it my business to see that you leave exactly as
you came—with nothing!'

'I wasn't aware that it *was* any of your business to see
how I came—or went,' snubbed Jade defiantly.

'Then that's where you made your first big mistake, isn't
it? because I shall be the next Mrs McGrath, and all your
fawning over Sarah and trying to get into Tory's good
graces will do you no good whatsoever! Once I'm mistress
here you will be *out*! Do you understand?'

'Oh, perfectly,' Jade concurred breezily, eyes opening
wide. 'But don't you think we should wait until that time
comes? After all, I don't see a ring on your finger yet,' she
challenged.

'It soon will be.' Laura sipped at her champagne indolently. 'I know for a fact that the family ring has been
sent to Brisbane for cleaning and a few minor alterations.'
She held her free hand before her, inspecting it imagin-
atively. 'Yes, I think those diamonds and emeralds will suit
me admirably, don't you?' she gibed.

Weary of the whole conversation and sick at heart with
the images it conjured up, Jade ignored her last question

174

and moved towards the door, longing for an escape from Laura's presence.

'Oh, Pascoe, that reminds me,' the other girl called after her in her most patronising tone, which had Jade struggling to hold her temper in check at the purposely denigrating usage of her surname. 'Sarah was talking about taking a few of the guests down to the museum. She asked me to tell you, if I happened to see you, to follow them down.'

Not trusting herself to speak, Jade nodded briefly and hurried out of the room, past the brilliantly thronged drawing room and out on to the refreshing coolness of the front verandah. For a moment she halted, drawing deep calming lungfuls of the invigorating air and glancing round at the trees ablaze with lights and the ornamental lanterns hanging from some of the lower boughs and casting complex patterns on the grass below.

Had she been a little clearer in her mind she might have found it extremely odd that Sarah had offered to take their guests down to the museum on this particular evening, but as it was she merely presumed that a few of them had imposed upon her to do so and Sarah had agreed rather than appear inhospitable.

However, the further she journeyed along the path the quieter it became—she would have expected to hear their voices before now—and she stopped hesitantly. At this distance from the house there were very few lights, and those that had been erected were only throwing fitful pools of light interspersed with great yawning stretches of darkness.

Another few steps took her further into the shadows once more and suddenly there loomed towards her from further down the path a man's dark shape. With a relieved laugh Jade hurried forward.

'Sarah's ahead of you, is she?' she questioned lightly.

'Why would I have Sarah with me? We want to be alone, don't we, sweetie?'

'Elliott!'

There was no mistaking those insolent accents and with a gasp of instinctive fear Jade turned to run, Laura's spitefully intent words, 'our turn will come' spoken at the picnic races beating at her ears. Why, they'd planned this between the two of them to get their own back. Sarah had never mentioned the museum!

'Come on, Jade, stop playing hard to get!' Elliott ordered impatiently, catching hold of her arm cruelly after only a few bounds and swinging her into the even darker shadows of a giant oak tree. 'You're no novice at this game!' he went on, adding insult to injury.

Desperately trying to pry herself loose from his tightening grasp, Jade threw at him heatedly, 'Whether I am or not, I'd still like the chance to choose my own partner, thanks very much, Elliott! This sort of tactic may have gone down well with your previous girl-friends, but I don't find it very appealing!'

'That's only because you won't let yourself,' he assured her, confident of his own powers of persuasion. 'Why don't you stop fighting and relax, sweetie?' as he edged her back against the hard trunk of the tree inexorably, twisting her arm behind her back while his free hand began to stroke the side of her neck coaxingly.

With her own free hand Jade knocked his away disgustedly, her nervousness increasing with the pressure of his body against her own, but trying not to panic she kept her voice cool.

'I'm sorry, Elliott, but I believe you must have misunderstood ordinary politeness for encouragement. I think you would agree that it would be better if you just let me go and we both forget all about this unpleasant incident,' she gave him a way out.

His first reaction was a burst of surprised laughter, followed by a deadly serious, 'You think I'm going to let you go after the trouble I went to to get you down here? That's a laugh,' he scoffed. 'You're going to find out that *no one* makes a fool of an Emery in public. It's going to give me a lot of pleasure making a little spitfire like you surrender.'

'*Never!*'

The word burst hotly from Jade's throat only seconds before Elliott's hand reached into her hair and wrenched her head back, preventing her from averting her face when his greedy mouth clamped down suffocatingly on to hers.

Filled with revulsion at his questing lips, Jade began to struggle furiously, beating and pushing at his arm and shoulder in her efforts to be free, but it wasn't until Elliott shifted his weight and let go of her hair in his attempt to penetrate the softly draped material of her neckline that she saw her opening and, with vicious intent, she raked her nails down the entire length of his face, from temple to chin.

Elliott sprang back with a shouted epithet, his hand automatically covering the three torn and scarlet furrows in his skin.

'You rotten little...!' he hissed at her through clenched teeth, and before Jade could realise what he intended, he had slapped her so resoundingly that she tumbled to the ground amidst the grass and leaves under the tree. Shock coursed through her system. No man had ever hit her before, and that thought, more than any actual pain caused by his blow, had her staring up at him wordlessly.

Elliott took another step towards her, but before he reached her another, larger shape appeared out of the blackness and he was almost spun completely off his feet as he was dragged around to face the newcomer. Then a powerful retaliatory backhand sent him, too, sprawling to the earth.

His livid fury all too visible even in the dim light, Tory now turned on Jade as the younger man began to climb groggily to his feet.

'You get yourself back to the house,' he ordered rawly. 'I'll deal with you when I've finished here!'

Only too pleased to be able to obey and leave such a humiliating scene, Jade scrambled to her feet, gathered her skirts into her hands and ran for the security of the homestead, where she entered by the back door and rushed unobserved up the stairs and into her room. Once safely inside she leant against the door, breathing heavily.

Again she had Tory to thank for a timely interference, but by the set of his features when she had left them on the pathway she didn't suppose she would be given the opportunity to explain her side of the incident. The fact that there had been no one else in the vicinity must seem, at least to Tory's eyes, to imply that she had gone with Elliott willingly.

She hunched her shoulders and abruptly came to a decision. Party or not, she was going into town! She certainly wasn't staying around for her third confrontation of the evening—first Laura, then Elliott—she wasn't going to be slated by Tory as well. With most of the local population at Marandoo tonight, she considered she ought to be able to find a nice quiet corner in Mac's hotel where she might more readily reassemble her shattered feelings.

In the bathroom she slipped off her dress, bespattered with twigs and leaves, and a hasty scrubbing of her face helped to wash away all traces of Elliott's unpleasant touch. Quickly she dressed in an old checked shirt and a pair of navy jeans and dragged some sandals on to her feet. Then, snatching her purse from the dressing table, she hurried across to the door.

A swift look in both directions and she was scurrying downstairs and out of the back door into the camper-van. Leaving the lights of the homestead fading rapidly behind her, Jade let go of the breath she had been unconsciously holding and lit a much-needed cigarette. She was sorry to have run out on Sarah in such a fashion, but she could not possibly have stayed and waited for the axe of Tory's wrath to fall—her nerves were in a bad enough state as it was.

Her foot pressed hard on the accelerator and she covered the miles into Wayamba in a very short time. Though the hotel was more patronised than she had expected, she managed to find herself a more or less secluded corner in front of the television. Mac served her himself with a brandy and lime, and although perhaps he wondered at her presence there alone, especially on such a night, he forbore to comment and Jade could have hugged him for his understanding. She wasn't in the mood for explanations!

When he brought her second drink he had looked at her a little strangely, she thought, but when he brought a third, the best part of an hour later, she concluded that she must have been imagining things, for he had regained his good spirits and placed the glass before her with his customary smile.

Shortly afterwards she heard Mac's voice raised in greeting from the bar and then Tory was standing in the doorway, his face dark and forbidding while his eyes glittered with an uncompromising light. His evening jacket and tie had been discarded, the top buttons of his shirt undone and the sleeves rolled up past his elbows. Jade stared at him in hypnotic quiescence—he looked so sensuously male!

Disregarding the startled glances cast at him by some of the other occupants of the lounge, he strode across the room purposefully, swept up Jade's belongings from the table and taking hold of her wrist in a no-nonsense grasp hauled her unceremoniously out of the chair and dragged her behind him, back past the now obviously interested clientele and out to his car parked beside the verandah. Still without having said a word he pulled open the passenger door, thrust Jade inside, shut it with a fiercely restrained action and paced around the vehicle to the driver's seat. The slam of his door made her flinch involuntarily and then the car was picking up speed and leaving the town swiftly in the rear.

Jade swallowed shakily and ventured a murmured recollection, 'My—my van...' which was totally ignored, and she subsided into a wary silence. The hour of reckoning had come and she didn't feel at all capable of defending herself.

A mile or so further down the road the car began to slow and Tory finally ran the vehicle off the bitumen and into a clearing beneath some trees. Jade could feel her muscles tightening nervously as she heard him turn the ignition off and swing to face her. Suddenly she knew she couldn't face him passively, her body was demanding action, and she flung open her door and then she was out of the car and running. Where she was going she had no idea—nor did she care—she only knew she couldn't just sit there and have him heap reproaches on her head.

By the time she realised his footsteps were close it was too late to dodge, and a muscular arm spanned her waist unexpectedly. Jade lost her footing, tripping Tory in the process, and together they rolled down the embankment away from the road and into the long grass. When their momentum had eased she fought to escape his grip but found herself pinned to the ground by a length of hard-sinewed body beside her that had no intention of allowing her to move.

'You stupid little idiot...' he breathed angrily, his eyes searing her with a glance and making Jade think inconsequentially that the moon must have been bright, for she could make out his face quite easily. 'Where the hell did you think you were going?'

Knowing she had to make some sort of a reply, Jade summoned her last reserves and jumped as impetuously as ever into the fray.

'I'm not necessarily an idiot, Tory, just because I don't always behave as you expect,' she retorted sarcastically.

'It doesn't make you a likely candidate for the Intelligence Corps, either!' he was quick to point out.

'Well, I didn't ask you to come chasing after me. I was quite happy where I was.'

180

'I'll bet you were! Especially since I'd already told you I wanted to see you at the house.'

'You surely didn't expect me to hang around there waiting for you to come and scold me like a schoolgirl in disgrace? It's not my fault if your girl-friend's brother can't take a hint when he's not wanted! She told me ...' Her voice died away as the age-old adage of 'don't tell tales' that had been drilled into her since childhood surged into her mind. She still had her own principles, even if others hadn't!

'I know, I know,' he repeated wearily, running a hand distractedly through his rumpled hair. '... that Sarah wanted you,' he finished for her. 'Don't worry, I've already had words with Laura over that little ruse.' His tone made Jade feel almost—but not quite—sorry for the girl. 'And, for your information, Laura is not my girl-friend and never has been,' he stated categorically.

A picture of Laura as Jade had last seen her sprang to mind, examining her fingers and gauging the effect that a certain ring would have on them.

'She certainly acts as though she is. It's always "darling" this and "darling" that,' she couldn't help grimacing.

'Which word you might have noticed I do not reciprocate! You wouldn't by any chance be jealous, would you?' he queried with a lazy smile hovering at the corners of his finely-shaped mouth.

The sudden thumping of her heart Jade felt would almost choke her and it was a formidable task she set herself to laugh lightly.

'Who, me? Hardly! I wouldn't expect you to be interested in a ...' she had been going to say 'nobody', but changed her mind, '... materialistic gold-digger like me!'

'Wouldn't you?' He ignored her uncomplimentary description. 'Not even when she happens to be one of the redhaired Pascoes who always manage to create such an upheaval whenever they set foot on Marandoo?' he finished with wry amusement.

181

'Especially not one of those!' she disallowed peremptorily, puzzled at the turn the conversation was taking when she had expected to be facing a barrage of criticism for her behaviour. She moved against his warm body restively.

'For heaven's sake, lie still, Jade!' she earned an explosive warning for her movement. 'The trouble with you is that you need someone to put a brand on you, honey. For your own protection ... as well as for every male's within a thirty-mile radius,' he informed her ruefully.

Jade's breathing deepened uncontrollably. 'And do you have any particular contenders picked out for my approval? Or will just anyone do?' she inquired tightly.

'Oh, no, not just anyone,' he disclosed with a smile that set her pulses racing. 'But yes, I do have someone in mind.'

'How very considerate of him to be willing to take on little ol' mercenary me!' she hurled at him, beginning to struggle in earnest now against those imprisoning arms. 'Well, as far as I'm concerned, you and your candidate can both go to hell! I don't need either of you to tell me when to get married, or to whom!' she panted between her exertions. 'I'm quite capable of deciding both of those things for myself, thank you!'

A smothered exclamation and Jade found her wrists locked in a relentless grip behind her back, a strong hand arresting her head and Tory's face inches from her own.

'And if you use those derogatory terms to describe yourself once more, I really will turn you over my knee!' he threatened.

'You used them first—I'm only repeating your own descriptions,' she reminded him tauntingly. 'You shouldn't find anything wrong in that.'

'Jade, for pity's sake, won't you stop fighting me just for once?' he appealed hoarsely.

She shook her head from side to side, biting at her lower lip. 'I can't,' she whispered faintly.

And it was true, for she was only too aware that if she

182

yielded she would be placing herself in a far more vulnerable position and one which would inflict only more misery and torment than did their continual verbal sparring.

'In that case, perhaps I'd better use another approach. This must be our only compatible ground!' Tory grated bitterly as his head lowered and his mouth found hers in a kiss that radiated a consuming fire in Jade's receptive bloodstream.

As always her response was instantaneous—something she could not withhold—her body arching into his invitingly and moving against him sinuously, while her lips returned his passionate mastery with a provocative desire of her own. Tory relinquished his hold on her wrists in order to gather her even closer into his masculine shape and Jade's responsive fingers slid tenderly from his waist along the sides of his deep chest and clasped across broad shoulders while she hungered for an even more expressive possession.

A moment later she was free and Tory moved away from her to sit with his arms resting across upraised knees, his head bowed.

'Dear God, Jade! You're tearing me apart!' he groaned huskily. 'Don't you know how much I want you? How much I love you?'

For a time Jade was unable to move—she couldn't believe it—she wouldn't let herself believe it! Then, quicker than she would have thought possible, she was on her knees beside him, gazing into his face.

'Tory?' she breathed hesitantly. 'Do you mean me?'

'Of course I mean you!' he asserted masterfully, pulling her back into his arms. 'How often do you think I leave my only sister's engagement party to go chasing over the countryside after one intractable female employee?'

All the love that Jade had been attempting to suppress for the last two weeks now came welling to the surface and she smiled enchantingly.

'That would depend on how often your sister becomes engaged,' she teased.

Tory's mouth effectively forestalled any further comments of a like nature and some long intoxicating moments passed before either of them spoke again.

'Will you marry me, Jade?' Tory broke the silence in impassioned tones.

With all her senses clamouring for her to say 'yes' unreservedly, Jade still kept a tight hold on her emotions.

'You did think once I was only interested in finding a wealthy husband,' she murmured, running a finger through the lacy ruffles of his shirt, 'and I'd hate you to ever think that again because, you see,' her eyes flickered shyly up to his and away again, 'money does burn a hole in my pocket. I know it's a bad habit and all that ... but I just can't help it,' she explained candidly. 'If I have any money I can't stop myself from spending it.'

Tory threw back his head and laughed, a richly devastating sound of untrammelled amusement.

'Darling, somehow I don't think even your pockets will be big enough to drain the family coffers, and I definitely will not ever think of you as an opportunist again. Does that satisfy you?'

'Oh, yes,' she sighed eloquently, her shining eyes giving him all the answer he could want. 'Of course I'll marry you, Tory. I love you too much to want ever to be parted from you.'

His arms hardened about her convulsively. 'And it had better be soon. I can't see myself surviving a long engagement,' he drawled wryly. 'You're far too much of a provocation, honey, and when I finally have the pleasure of taking you to my bed I'd prefer it to be within the bonds of matrimony.'

Jade flushed to a becoming rose colour and nestled her head deeper into his shoulder.

'So the McGraths and the Pascoes are to make a match of it after all,' she mused aloud.

'You surely didn't doubt it? Why, even as far back as the night I first saw you I knew there had to be *something* between us.' A gentle finger traced the outline of her enticing mouth. 'The only time I ever doubted our future was when I saw you disappearing beneath the rapids. That experience took years off my life—I never thought I'd reach you in time,' he confessed.

'Why didn't you say anything before now?'

A lazy grin made its appearance. 'Because every time I spoke to you, you erected a wall of verbal defence between us that was so high it would have taken an Edmund Hillary to scale it. The only encouragement I ever received was when I kissed you,' he smiled down at her reminiscently. 'Even tonight you made it perfectly clear that you considered I had no right to comment on your hair.'

'How could I?' Jade turned questioning eyes upwards. 'I still thought you believed I was looking for easy riches and I was scared stiff of what you might say if you discovered I was in love with you. Then, when you shouted at me after you hit Elliott, I couldn't take any more. I had to get away by myself for a while.'

'And have me going out of my mind trying to find you,' he laughed, and pulled at one of her bright curls punishingly. 'It was only as a last resort that I phoned Mac to see if you might be at the hotel,' which explained that gentleman's odd look when delivering her second drink, 'and I was picturing all sorts of devious ways in which to make sure you honoured our contract. I thought it was more than likely that you intended leaving altogether.'

That he should have gone to such lengths spread a pleased smile over Jade's face. 'Why did you make me sign that contract, Tory?' she probed interestedly. 'You didn't make Helen sign one.'

'As I told you, I'd already sensed there would be some-

185

thing between us and I thought that might be a way to ensure you were around long enough for me to find out exactly what I really did feel about you. You see, I'd been watching you for some time that night in the hotel and I thought you were too beautiful to be true.' His face was rueful. 'I rather think my first feelings were plain old-fashioned jealousy when I saw you laughing with Gary and Mike, so when you made that comment about looking for a wealthy husband I was only too pleased to have a reason for mistrusting you. A belated form of self-preservation, I guess,' he admitted. 'That's why I had Sarah conduct your initial interview—feeling as I did, I might have refused to employ you. Somehow I think I must have sensed that Sarah would like you and, therefore, take the decision out of my hands.'

'You didn't appear as though you appreciated having had the decision made for you,' she pointed out mischievously. 'You were furious that day when I walked into your office.'

'By then I'd managed to work myself up into a state of righteous indignation, and thereafter I almost persuaded myself it was the truth. Especially when you kept agreeing with me, you little troublemaker!'

Jade slipped her arms about his neck and trailed warm lips tantalisingly down the tanned skin to the base of his throat.

'See, even that long ago I was only trying to please you,' she tormented in a husky voice.

'The trouble is, you please me too much,' he groaned, and cupping her face between two hands he set his lips to hers in a fiery brand of possession that she yielded to with a sensuous surrender.

'Come on, honey,' Tory gruffly broke their embrace, his hand a little unsteady as it sought hers and he reluctantly pulled them both to their feet. 'Much more of this and I can see myself not being able to refrain from making love to you right here and now! I think it's about time we put in a

186

reappearance at Barbara's party. I should be called upon to make an announcement very shortly.'

Pressed close to his side, Jade darted a nervous glance upwards as they walked slowly down the road to the car.

'Do you think Sarah and Barbara will be annoyed with me for having taken you away from the party?' she asked.

'Not when they know the outcome,' he smiled at her gently. 'Sarah's been your greatest advocate ever since you arrived, and Barbara will be only too pleased to see me leaving what she calls my "worthless bachelorhood" behind. I'm sure the whole family will be very happy to have you join the clan.'

'And Laura and Elliott?' she had to ask.

'After the words we had, I doubt whether Laura will be overly anxious to be visiting the property for many months to come. As for Elliott, I could quite cheerfully have killed him when I saw him slap you.' A tender hand smoothed against her cheek. 'Does it still hurt?'

Jade shook her head carelessly. 'No, not any more. I've had more important things on my mind,' she confessed with a bewitching smile.

'Well, you certainly gave *him* something to think about,' Tory grinned in remembrance. 'That was one hell of a brand you left on his face. I guess I should consider myself lucky I didn't receive the same treatment.'

'Oh, no, it never occurred to me,' she assured him earnestly before a bubbling laugh sprang to the surface. 'I *liked* being kissed by you!' which was rewarded by a heart-stopping smile. Then, more seriously, 'But I did think it was unfair of you to suggest I might like to visit the museum at night with Elliott—*that* I didn't appreciate!'

'A small touch of McGrath vengeance,' he admitted readily. 'I'd kissed you for the first time that afternoon and found myself wanting more ... much more! I figured that if you went with Elliott then I was right in my surmise—

you didn't care who it was, as long as they had money. I'm pleased to say I was wrong!'

As he opened the car door for her Jade swung round and slid her arms around his waist, holding him close.

'I'm glad you were too, because I love you, Tory, more than I can ever say. It would have broken my heart to leave when those three months were up.'

Safe within the circle of his protecting arms she heard his deep voice close beside her ear.

'By then I couldn't have let you go. As Reid so aptly predicted ... when I fell, I fell hard!'

And so, with a bright new moon to guide them, another redheaded Pascoe and a dark McGrath journeyed back to Marandoo, where it had all begun so many long years ago.

Did you miss any of these exciting Harlequin Omnibus 3-in-1 volumes?

Each volume contains 3 great novels by one author for only $1.95.
See order coupon.

Violet Winspear

Violet Winspear #3
The Cazalet Bride (#1434)
Beloved Castaway (#1472)
The Castle of the Seven Lilacs (#1514)

Anne Mather

Anne Mather
Charlotte's Hurricane (#1487)
Lord of Zaracus (#1574)
The Reluctant Governess (#1600)

Anne Hampson

Anne Hampson #1
Unwary Heart (#1388)
Precious Waif (#1420)
The Autocrat of Melhurst (#1442)

Betty Neels

Betty Neels
Tempestuous April (#1441)
Damsel in Green (#1465)
Tulips for Augusta (#1529)

Essie Summers

Essie Summers #3
Summer in December (#1416)
The Bay of the Nightingales (#1445)
Return to Dragonshill (#1502)

Margaret Way

Margaret Way
King Country (#1470)
Blaze of Silk (#1500)
The Man from Bahl Bahla (#1530)

---

40 magnificent Omnibus volumes to choose from:

Essie Summers #1
Bride in Flight (#933)
Postscript to Yesterday (#1119)
Meet on My Ground (#1326)

Jean S. MacLeod
The Wolf of Heimra (#990)
Summer Island (#1314)
Slave of the Wind (#1339)

Eleanor Farnes
The Red Cliffs (#1335)
The Flight of the Swan (#1280)
Sister of the Housemaster (#975)

Susan Barrie #1
Marry a Stranger (#1034)
Rose in the Bud (#1168)
The Marriage Wheel (#1311)

Violet Winspear #1
Beloved Tyrant (#1032)
Court of the Veils (#1267)
Palace of the Peacocks (#1318)

Isobel Chace
The Saffron Sky (#1250)
A Handful of Silver (#1306)
The Damask Rose (#1334)

Joyce Dingwell #1
Will You Surrender (#1179)
A Taste for Love (#1229)
The Feel of Silk (#1342)

Sara Seale
Queen of Hearts (#1324)
Penny Plain (#1197)
Green Girl (#1045)

Jane Arbor
A Girl Named Smith (#1000)
Kingfisher Tide (#950)
The Cypress Garden (#1336)

Anne Weale
The Sea Waif (#1123)
The Feast of Sara (#1007)
Doctor in Malaya (#914)

Essie Summers #2
His Serene Miss Smith (#1093)
The Master to Tawhai (#910)
A Place Called Paradise (#1156)

Catherine Airlie
Doctor Overboard (#979)
Nobody's Child (#1258)
A Wind Sighing (#1328)

Violet Winspear #2
Bride's Dilemma (#1008)
Tender Is the Tyrant (#1208)
The Dangerous Delight (#1344)

Kathryn Blair
Doctor Westland (#954)
Battle of Love (#1038)
Flowering Wilderness (#1148)

Rosalind Brett
The Girl at White Drift (#1101)
Winds of Enchantment (#1176)
Brittle Bondage (#1319)

Rose Burghley
Man of Destiny (#960)
The Sweet Surrender (#1023)
The Bay of Moonlight (#1245)

Iris Danbury
Rendezvous in Lisbon (#1178)
Doctor at Villa Ronda (#1257)
Hotel Belvedere (#1331)

Amanda Doyle
A Change for Clancy (#1085)
Play the Tune Softly (#1116)
A Mist in Glen Torran (#1308)

Great value in Reading!
Use the handy order form

Elizabeth Hoy
Snare the Wild Heart
(#992)
The Faithless One
(#1104)
Be More than Dreams
(#1286)

Roumelia Lane
House of the Winds
(#1262)
A Summer to Love
(#1280)
Sea of Zanj (#1338)

Margaret Malcolm
The Master of
Normanhurst (#1028)
The Man in Homespun
(#1140)
Meadowsweet (#1164)

Joyce Dingwell #2
The Timber Man (#917)
Project Sweetheart
(#964)
Greenfingers Farm
(#999)

Marjorie Norell
Nurse Madeline of Eden
Grove (#962)
Thank You, Nurse
Conway (#1097)
The Marriage of Doctor
Royle (#1177)

Anne Durham
New Doctor at
Northmoor (#1242)
Nurse Sally's Last
Chance (#1281)
Mann of the Medical
Wing (#1313)

Henrietta Reid
Reluctant Masquerade
(#1380)
Hunter's Moon (#1430)
The Black Delaney
(#1460)

Lucy Gillen
The Silver Fishes
(#1408)
Heir to Glen Ghyll
(#1450)
The Girl at Smuggler's
Rest (#1533)

Anne Hampson #2
When the Bough Breaks
(#1491)
Love Hath an Island
(#1522)
Stars of Spring (#1551)

Essie Summers #4
No Legacy for Lindsay
(#957)
No Orchids by Request
(#982)
Sweet Are the Ways
(#1015)

Mary Burchell #3
The Other Linding Girl
(#1431)
Girl with a Challenge
(#1455)
My Sister Celia (#1474)

Susan Barrie #2
Return to Tremarth
(#1359)
Night of the Singing
Birds (#1428)
Bride in Waiting
(#1526)

Violet Winspear #4
Desert Doctor (#921)
The Viking Stranger
(#1080)
The Tower of the Captive
(#1111)

Essie Summers #5
Heir to Windrush Hill
(#1055)
Rosalind Comes Home
(#1283)
Revolt — and Virginia
(#1348)

Doris E. Smith
To Sing Me Home
(#1427)
Seven of Magpies
(#1454)
Dear Deceiver (#1599)

Katrina Britt
Healer of Hearts
(#1393)
The Fabulous Island
(#1490)
A Spray of Edelweiss
(#1626)

Betty Neels #2
Sister Peters in
Amsterdam (#1361)
Nurse in Holland
(#1385)
Blow Hot — Blow Cold
(#1409)

Amanda Doyle #2
The Girl for Gillgong
(#1351)
The Year at Yattabilla
(#1448)
Kookaburra Dawn
(#1562)

Complete and mail this coupon today!